# The
# Knotted Rope

OTHER BOOKS
BY JEAN RAE BAXTER

*Hope's Journey*
Ronsdale Press, 2015

*The White Oneida*
Ronsdale Press, 2014

*Respectable Appearance*
Marenga Publishers (Tel Aviv), 2013

*Freedom Bound*
Ronsdale Press, 2012

*Broken Trail*
Ronsdale Press, 2011

*Scattered Light*
Seraphim Editions, 2011

*Looking for Cardenio*
Seraphim Editions, 2008

*The Way Lies North*
Ronsdale Press, 2007

*A Twist of Malice*
Seraphim Editions, 2005

# The
# Knotted Rope

**JEAN RAE BAXTER**

RONSDALE PRESS

THE KNOTTED ROPE
Copyright © 2021 Jean Rae Baxter

RONSDALE PRESS
3350 West 21st Avenue, Vancouver, B.C. Canada V6S 1G7
www.ronsdalepress.com

Typesetting: Julie Cochrane, in Minion 12 pt on 16
Cover Design: Nancy de Brouwer, Massive Graphic Design
Paper: 100 Edition, 60 lb. offset white paper (FSC)—100% post-consumer waste, totally chlorine-free and acid-free.

Ronsdale Press wishes to thank the following for their support of its publishing program: the Canada Council for the Arts, the Government of Canada, the British Columbia Arts Council, and the Province of British Columbia through the British Columbia Book Publishing Tax Credit program.

**Library and Archives Canada Cataloguing in Publication**

Title: The knotted rope / Jean Rae Baxter.
Names: Baxter, Jean Rae, author.
Identifiers: Canadiana (print) 2021030202X | Canadiana (ebook) 20210321091 | ISBN 9781553806202 (softcover) | ISBN 9781553806219 (ebook) | ISBN 9781553806226 (PDF)
Subjects: LCSH: Slavery—Canada—Juvenile fiction. | LCSH: Canada—History—1763–1867—Juvenile fiction.
Classification: LCC PS8603.A935 K66 2021 | DDC jC813/.6—dc23

At Ronsdale Press we are committed to protecting the environment. To this end we are working with Canopy and printers to phase out our use of paper produced from ancient forests. This book is one step towards that goal.

Printed in Canada by Island Blue, Victoria, B.C.

*in memory of*
*Jill Fiander*

ACKNOWLEDGEMENTS

Foremost among those who helped me tell this tale is Dr. Leigh Smith, retired professor in the Department of Geology at Queen's University. A sedimentary geologist, knowing more than I could ask or imagine about limestone, he was an ever-obliging source of knowledge about the geology of the Niagara Escarpment and the history of Niagara Falls through the millennia. He also, as the first reader of every draft, saved the book from overloaded verbiage. Closely behind stands my publisher at Ronsdale Press, Ronald Hatch. His counsel and guidance pointed the way and kept me going. Veronica Hatch and Meagan Dyer, also of Ronsdale Press provided much-needed editorial advice through various revisions. My thanks are also due to John Stuart Haberl Baxter for technical computer support and to other Baxters for help of many kinds.

By the middle of the seventeenth century, the institution of slavery was well-established in the Americas. Fortunes were made through the transportation of Africans as slaves to North America, South America and the Caribbean. Most of the slaves came from the West Coast of Africa.

The captured Africans were carried like cargo below the deck, tied down in rows, confined in darkness and barely able to move. Of the fifteen million black Africans loaded onto the slave ships, three million died during the crossing.

In 1772 slavery ended in England. It was not abolished. No new law was passed. The end of slavery in England resulted from a legal judgment in a case called the Somersett Case. James Somersett was a slave brought back to England by a British customs official named Charles Stewart, who had bought him in Boston. Once in England, Somersett escaped. He was recaptured. His owner imprisoned him on a ship that was to sail to Jamaica, where he would be sold to work on a plantation. Abolitionists applied to the Court of King's Bench for a writ of *habeas corpus*. In a famous judgement, Lord Mansfield ruled in 1772 that since neither Common Law nor Statute Law nor Natural Law supported the institution of slavery, "the man must be discharged."

In effect, this meant that the 14,000 slaves currently owned in England became free. Henceforth no person could be a slave in

England. But this did not prevent English entrepreneurs from participating in the slave trade.

The Abolitionist Movement in Britain raised awareness of the cruelty involved in the slave trade. Yet, despite its efforts, it was not until 1807 that an Act of Parliament abolished the slave trade, and not until 1833 that slavery itself was abolished throughout the British Empire.

The American Congress also abolished the slave trade in 1807. Although this put slave traders out of business, it had little effect on slavery in America. American slave owners by this time had built up a so-called domestic breeding stock. It took the defeat of the South in the American Civil War in 1865 to bring an end to slavery in the United States.

There were two kinds of slave auction: an auction of newly imported Africans fresh off the boat, and a domestic auction of slaves already in the colony. The usual practice was to separate the slaves by sex and line them up in order of height. The ones straight from Africa were destined to work on plantations. They were exhibited almost naked, their skins oiled to give a healthy appearance.

A wealthy family often purchased a baby slave for their own baby. The two would grow up together, each knowing his or her place. A boy would grow up to be his young master's valet, a girl to be her mistress' lady's maid.

There were two kinds of slaves: field slaves and house slaves. The lives of field slaves were much the same whether the plantation owning them produced sugar or cotton or rice or indigo. The slaves lived in huts, windows barred and doors locked at night to prevent escape.

It was an advancement for a slave to be taken from the labour of the fields to become a house slave. A girl could be trained in many skills: cooking, washing and ironing, soap-making and candle-making. A young woman might be apprenticed to a dress-maker. Martha Washington owned the dressmaker who made her beautiful gowns.

A young man could learn to wait at table. Wealthy families took pride in dressing their male servants in satin livery with ruffled shirts. A well-trained slave was an investment. An owner might spend a lot of money apprenticing a likely boy to a carpenter or cabinet maker. Then he would have a skilled craftsman to hire out. You could teach a slave a trade, but not how to read and write.

It was common for the master and his sons to have sexual rela-tions with female slaves. This led to the production of half-black children. Mulattos. The next generation would be quadroons, then octoroons. Of an octoroon's eight great-grandparents, only one was of African descent, but the octoroon was still a slave.

Harsh measures were taken to keep slaves under control. In Charleston, punishment was frequently a visit to the House of Correction. The Workhouse "whipping room" was constructed of double walls filled with sand to muffle the screams of inmates. It housed a crane, "on which a cord with two nooses ran over pulleys." The warden chained the feet of slaves to bolts in the floor, and then hoisted the crane until their bodies were "stretched out as much as possible."

In 1775, the year when hostilities began in the American War of Independence, there were 2½ million people of British and other European descent in North America. There were also 470,000 African North Americans, of whom 95% were slaves.

Most of the free 5% had been given their freedom under their master's will. The rest had earned it. There were benevolent masters who allowed their slaves to seek odd jobs when their own work was done. In that way a slave could save the money to buy his freedom.

The story of the Black Loyalists begins with Britain's offer of freedom to slaves owned by Patriots. Basically, it was a stratagem for upsetting the economy of the rebelling Southern Colonies. A guarantee of freedom called the General Birch Certificate was awarded to any rebel-owned slave who escaped behind British lines and served the military for one full year. A man might serve in the Black Pioneers or the Black Dragoons, or he might just work as a stable boy. A woman might earn her certificate by working as a laundress or as a cook for an officer.

As many as 30,000 slaves had escaped to British lines by October 1781 when the British General Charles Cornwallis surrendered his troops at Yorktown, Virginia. Faithful to their promise, the British drew up a list of all who had earned the General Birch Certificate. To save their lives as well as their freedom, they had to be evacuated. Their names and circumstances were recorded in a unique ledger known as *The Book of Negroes*. Mandated by Sir Guy Carleton, the British commander-in-chief, it listed peoples' ages, physical condition, and colonies of origin. *The Book of Negroes* has become an invaluable source of information about the Black Loyalists.

Some of the evacuation ships went to East Florida and the West Indies, some to England, and others to Nova Scotia. White Loyalists and their slaves as well as free Black Loyalists would frequently all be passengers on the same ship.

Loyalist Colonel John Butler's regiment, "Butler's Rangers," included black as well as white soldiers. All received equal treatment. After the war ended, Colonel Butler settled his Rangers on land grants along the West Bank of the Niagara River in Upper Canada.

Because of the Somersett judgment, any black who set foot in England would be automatically free. But what of the much larger number who went to British North America? In that case, the slaves who belonged to Loyalists were still slaves, and their owners had no intention of giving them up. Loyalists who owned slaves brought their property with them when they settled in Halifax, Saint John, Quebec, Montreal, Niagara, York and Kingston.

Joseph Brant (Thayendanegea) owned slaves. Some were house slaves. He also owned about forty-five men who were used mainly in construction.

Upper Canada was the first jurisdiction in the British Empire to pass a law limiting slavery. This was due to the efforts of Lieutenant-Governor John Graves Simcoe. He was an abolitionist.

Simcoe had to proceed cautiously. Possibly one-third of the members of the Legislature were slave owners. They had a big financial investment.

In the statute that came into law in Upper Canada in 1793, "No Negro or other person . . . brought into this Province shall be subject to the condition of slavery." The new law also provided that children born to female slaves must be freed at age twenty-five. Disappointed at his failure to abolish slavery completely, Simcoe took solace in the fact that those who remained slaves "may henceforth look forward to the emancipation of their offspring."

Few owners wanted the expense of bringing up a child who must be set free at twenty-five, just when becoming most valuable.

As a result, some Upper Canadians freed their slaves. Others took them to the States and sold them. In 1790 there were about 300 slaves in Upper Canada. By 1810, thanks to Simcoe's efforts, few were left.

Relatively few Black Loyalists went to Nova Scotia. In the years following the American Revolution, there were 1,200 of them. The settlement they lived in was called Birchtown, receiving that name from the General Birch Certificate.

The General Birch Certificate that gave them their freedom also gave them the most barren land in Nova Scotia. Some died from the harsh winters. Even worse, the white population turned against them. The Black Loyalists flocked into towns, looking for work. But there were also hundreds of disbanded white soldiers needing employment. The blacks would work for less. Thus they were accused of stealing white jobs. There was a riot, in which many blacks were badly beaten.

After ten miserable years the Black Loyalists of Nova Scotia petitioned the British government to resettle them in Africa. The Sierra Leone Company had been founded in England to establish a colony in Sierra Leone to relocate former slaves. In 1792, 1,196 Black Loyalists sailed from Halifax to Sierra Leone in fifteen ships. They called their settlement Freetown. The descendants of these Black Loyalists form an important element of the population of Freetown today.

# The
# Knotted Rope

# Prologue

A woman's shrieks ripped through the silence. She was black and she fought like a trapped beast. Feet, knees, fists, arms, teeth. Terror in her eyes. Three white men held her down. Grunting, cursing, trying to tie a rope around her ankles. Their boat waited, bobbing on the slushy water among the chunks of broken ice.

Broken Trail gripped the handle of his tomahawk. He had to help that woman. He was ready to attack. But if he used the tomahawk, he might strike her as she writhed and struggled to escape. No weapon then. Just his bare hands. He sprang like a cougar, wrapping his arm around one man's neck. But there were three, and they were tough, muscular men. One pulled him off and sent him flying with a blow to the head.

He rose from his hands and knees, his mind and body burning to fight again. But it was too late. The men had the woman tied. She was trussed like a chicken and still shrieking as they threw her into their boat. They jumped in and took up oars. The boat pulled away across the Niagara River.

When Broken Trail turned his head, he saw that he was not the only witness. Two men, one white and the other black, stood watching him. They were not young, but not old, either. Their steady gaze suggested the resolve of experienced soldiers who knew when to fight and when to draw back. They walked up to Broken Trail.

"You can't help her that way," said the white bystander. "The law is against you."

"What law?"

"The law that makes that woman a piece of property. She's a slave. Her owner has the right to take her over to New York State and sell her. If you were caught fighting to free her, it's you who'd go to jail."

Broken Trail, still groggy, shook his head. "If that's the law, then it must be changed."

The black man nodded. "That's what we think, too." He paused. "You look ready for a fight. Do you want to help us change the law?"

"Leave the young fellow alone." The white man's eyes

moved from Broken Trail's scalp lock to his leather poncho and to his breechcloth and buckskin leggings. "Can't you see he's half Indian? Slavery isn't his problem. This is not his fight."

"Maybe it is my fight. I was born white but raised Oneida. Think of how the Native people have been treated. I've seen a lot of injustice in my life."

The woman was still screaming, but the clamour lessened as the boat pulled further away.

The white man sighed. "I'll tell you something. There are plenty of people in Upper Canada who want to end slavery. But the rich people who control the government are the ones who own slaves. They don't want any change."

"Except for the Lieutenant-Governor," the black man added. "Simcoe is rich, but he's an abolitionist. He's just waiting for a chance to end slavery in this province."

"This may be the chance he's waiting for." The white man raised his eyes to the river, where the boat was halfway to the far shore. The woman's screams were fainter now. "If Simcoe hears about this, it may be the spur he needs to put pressure on the government."

"I'm on my way to Newark to see Governor Simcoe." Broken Trail brushed off his leggings, which were dirty from the struggle. "I can report what we saw."

"We should go with you," the black man said. "Three witnesses are better than one. We can be at Simcoe's headquarters in less than an hour."

"Let's do it." Broken Trail picked up his rifle, hoisted his carrying basket onto his back and walked with them as they climbed the slope from the Queenston landing place and turned east on the road to Newark.

# CHAPTER 1

# The War Chief's Deputy

Broken Trail's companions said their names: Peter Martin, with skin as brown as a hickory nut, and Will Grisley, who wore a short bristle of yellow whiskers on his pink cheeks. They walked three abreast, the mud sucking at Broken Trail's moccasins and at his companions' boots. The road to Newark ran along the bank of the Niagara Gorge. On their right, far below them, flowed the dark water of the Niagara River, dotted with chunks of ice. On their left, patches of snow still lay on the fields. Loyalist settlers had cleared these fields. Deep furrows, made by their ploughs in the fall to prepare the ground for spring planting, curved around the rotting tree stumps.

"Do you live near here?" Broken Trail asked.

"We do," said Grisley. "Each of us owns one hundred acres."

"We're both old soldiers, veterans of Butler's Rangers," Martin added. "Some Rangers were black like me, and some were white. Colonel Butler treated us all alike. After the war, when veterans were given land grants, he made sure black and white got exactly the same."

"The new Lieutenant-Governor wants to take equality one final step further." Grisley glanced around, but the road was empty apart from them. "No more slavery."

Broken Trail raised his eyebrows. "That's a giant step."

As they talked, they tramped the seven miles to Newark past farms and woodlots, through the village of Newark and down a hill to a cluster of old wooden buildings near a wharf, where the Niagara River flowed into Lake Ontario.

Grisley pointed to the buildings. "That's Navy Hall."

Broken Trail took in their run-down frontage, confused. "They look like barracks."

"They are barracks. Governor Simcoe uses one as his headquarters."

Broken Trail thought this a poor-looking place for a Lieutenant-Governor to have his headquarters, but the sharp appearance of the soldier on duty at the door, with his smart red coat and tall shako hat, made up for the deficiency.

After hearing why they wanted to see the Governor, the soldier told them to wait while he told Simcoe their purpose.

After a few minutes, the door opened and the soldier ushered them inside. Lieutenant-Governor Simcoe rose from his desk to welcome them.

Simcoe wore a red coat with gold epaulets at the shoulders and masses of gold braid. Everything about him looked crisp and military. As he learned about the cruel treatment of the slave woman, he shook his head angrily. "I will investigate this matter. If the woman's owner acted legally, the law must be changed."

After Simcoe had thanked them for reporting the abuse, Broken Trail spoke up. "Sir, I must ask for a few more minutes of your time. I was sent here on a separate matter. When I witnessed what happened at Queenston Landing, I was on official business. I serve as deputy for Thayendanegea—I mean, Captain Joseph Brant—the war chief of the Mohawk Nation. I have brought you his report on the recent conference of war chiefs that took place at Buffalo Creek."

"Indeed, that is also a matter of grave importance. The Native people as well as the enslaved Africans have been unjustly treated." Simcoe took the paper from Broken Trail's hand. "I'll give Captain Brant's report my full attention. Did he ask you to wait for my reply?"

"No, sir. My instructions were to deliver his report and then return to Brant's Ford."

"Then I wish you a safe return." He turned his head to include the others. "I thank all of you for coming here to tell me about the abuse of the slave woman."

After leaving Simcoe's headquarters, Broken Trail and his companions wished each other well and went their separate ways.

. . .

Three days later, at sundown, Broken Trail reached Thayendanegea's home at Brant's Ford. He unlatched the gate on the white picket fence, went around to the back of the house and entered by the kitchen door. There was Sophia Pooley, Thayendanegea's slave, standing at the fireplace, turning the crank that rotated the roasting pig on the spit. The smell made Broken Trail's mouth water.

"You're back!" Sophia smiled. "Dinner's almost ready."

"First I must wash and change my clothes. I can't present myself to Thayendanegea's family looking like this." From head to foot, his clothes were smeared with mud and grime.

"Your room's ready. I'll bring hot water for you to wash."

Broken Trail went straight to his room, which was just down the hall from the kitchen, not upstairs with the family's bedrooms.

Thayendanegea's house had a stone cellar and clapboard exterior walls joined by hand-wrought nails. Plastered walls and painted floors covered by woven rugs made the interior feel bright and modern. But in the yard behind the house was a sweat lodge, clad with sheets of elm bark. As Thayendanegea frequently boasted, he enjoyed the best of two worlds.

Sophia brought Broken Trail a large pitcher of hot water, which she poured into the china basin on his washstand. She left him with a bar of yellow soap, a flannel and a soft towel. After a week wearing the same clothes, he was impatient to strip them off.

An hour later, Broken Trail was washed and dressed in a clean red-and-black-checkered shirt, red neckerchief and creamy deerskin leggings. Leaving his room, he heard children's voices coming from outdoors and their mother Catharine's voice calling to them. He went directly to the library, where Thayendanegea rose from his armchair beside the fireplace.

"Welcome back! Sophia told me you had returned. Dinner is ready. You can tell me later about your journey. I want to hear everything."

*Everything? Even what happened to the woman slave?* The idea made Broken Trail uneasy, but he nodded as though this would be no trouble at all.

In the dining room, Thayendanegea took his place at the head of the table, with Catharine on his right and Broken Trail on his left. Next to Broken Trail sat nine-year-old Joseph Junior, across from his brother Jacob, who was seven. The boys wore linsey-woolsey shirts such as any white schoolboy might wear, but their chin-length hair was held back by a headband of bright beadwork. Catharine wore a blue gown of fine wool trimmed with lace. Her lustrous black hair was dressed in the Mohawk style for a married woman, with a single braid down the back looped up underneath and tied with a ribbon.

Sophia carried from the kitchen platters of roast pork and corn cakes and bowls of boiled potatoes, mashed turnips and stewed beaver. When everything was in place, she stood back from the table to serve the family. Unobtrusively, she watched to see whose glass needed refilling and who was ready for a second helping of food.

Broken Trail had just finished his corn cakes when she stepped forward and placed more on his plate. "Thank you."

"It's not necessary to thank her," Thayendanegea grunted. "She's a slave."

"I thank her to show my appreciation. Slaves are people, just like us."

"They're people, I agree, but they're not like us. We own them. That's something they mustn't forget."

"I don't see how they could forget." Broken Trail's face grew hot.

A few minutes later, Sophia stepped forward to refill his water glass. "Thank you," he said firmly.

Thayendanegea scowled. Catharine gasped. Joseph Junior and Jacob giggled.

After a pause, Catharine changed the subject. "Spring will soon be here. When the snow melts, I'll go to the forest to gather bloodroot and hepatica to make medicines."

"The sap is already running. I have a crew of slaves tapping maple trees." Thayendanegea turned to his sons. "Boys, we'll be having maple syrup on our corn cakes before long." Then he gave Broken Trail a hard look. "I hope you don't object to maple syrup made by slave labour?"

"I object to anything made by slave labour."

Catharine gave him a pained look, obviously unsettled by his refusal to drop the subject. They finished the meal in silence.

• • •

The weeks crawled by, shaped by work. There were many letters for Thayendanegea and Broken Trail to write. These letters were to government officials and other important men. They dealt with treaty rights and land settlement. This work was as important to Broken Trail as it was to Thayendanegea. Both sought justice for the Native people. Why was Thayendanegea blind to the even greater injustice done to the enslaved blacks? That was the question Broken Trail never stopped asking himself.

He continued to eat with the family, and at every meal he continued to thank Sophia whenever she refilled his water glass or his plate. Thayendanegea scowled at first, but eventually decided to ignore Broken Trail's persistence. Catharine, as well, seemed no longer to notice it. As for Joseph Junior and Jacob, they stopped giggling and even gave sly smiles, as if they approved of Broken Trail's words of thanks to kindly Sophia.

• • •

Three months passed. It was July when Thayendanegea summoned him to his library to give him a new assignment.

"I'm sending you back to Newark with an invitation for Lieutenant-Governor Simcoe to pay a formal visit to Brant's Ford. You will leave tomorrow." He handed a letter to Broken Trail. It was addressed to Lieutenant-Governor John Graves Simcoe.

"I'll be ready to leave at dawn."

"After you have delivered my letter, bring back his reply."

Broken Trail went to his room to pack his carrying basket, putting into it his best clothes and a spare pair of moccasins. He looked forward to the journey. In the forest, he could do everything for himself—make his own bed of spruce boughs, light his own campfire, cook his own meal over the flames. But this mission was especially important to him because it would give him an opportunity to learn of any progress Simcoe was making in the fight against slavery, and how he could help.

CHAPTER 2

# A Visit to Mr. Steele

✥

Four days later, Broken Trail stood in front of Simcoe's desk at the Lieutenant-Governor's headquarters at Navy Hall. Simcoe looked pale, the skin puffy about his eyes as if he had not slept well.

"Sir," announced Broken Trail, "I've just arrived from Brant's Ford with a letter for you from Captain Joseph Brant."

"Just arrived, eh? Let's see the letter." As Simcoe took it from Broken Trail's hand, he looked closely at him. "Haven't I seen you before?"

"I was here in March to deliver Captain Brant's report on the Six Nations Conference at Buffalo Creek."

"I remember the report. But that's not the only reason I remember you. You came with two other witnesses to tell me about the abuse of a slave named Chloe Cooley."

"I didn't know her name."

"By now, almost everybody in this province knows her name. That poor woman—treated like merchandise! *This has to stop!* I told myself. Slavery ended twenty-one years ago in England when Lord Mansfield's judgment made it illegal. It's a disgrace that this evil still exists in the rest of the British Empire." Simcoe shrugged. "I can't do much about the Empire, but I'm determined to abolish slavery in this province. My critics say I'm neglecting my responsibilities as Lieutenant-Governor. As an abolitionist, I have no choice."

After this outburst, Simcoe cleared his throat. "Excuse me. You've brought me a letter from Captain Brant. Please take a seat while I read it."

Broken Trail shrugged his carrying basket from his back, leaned his rifle against the wall and sat down on a chair while Simcoe cracked the seal and unfolded the paper. As he read, he shook his head.

"Captain Brant invites me to visit him at Brant's Ford. I stayed there in February for a few days. It was quite a journey, mostly on snowshoes. He showed me the new church and the school."

"He's eager to show you more of the improvements he has made. If you visit him now, you can see the fields of corn and wheat and the grist mill in operation. He'll take you fishing on the Grand River."

"Captain Brant was a most pleasant host. His slaves waited on me hand and foot. He told me he has forty-five slaves. He's proud of that." Simcoe frowned. "We had an interesting discussion about slavery. Interesting, but not pleasant. Maybe that's why he wants me to return, so he can try again to convince me that slavery is both good and necessary."

"I can't presume to guess his purpose."

"Perhaps I'm too suspicious." Simcoe refolded the letter. "Even if I wanted to, I can't go now. This is a critical time. Tomorrow, the new law limiting slavery receives Royal Assent."

"What does that mean?"

"Under my hand and seal as the King's representative, the new law takes effect tomorrow. As of July 9, 1793, any child born to a slave must be set free at age twenty-five. Just as important, the new law stops people from bringing slaves into this province. The moment a slave sets foot in Upper Canada, he becomes free. These two provisions will gradually eliminate slavery in this province."

"Why gradually? Why not do it now?"

"Unfortunately, the new law won't free people who are enslaved right now. You see, two-thirds of the men in the Legislative Assembly and the Executive Council are slave owners. It was hard work persuading them to put any limits on slavery. The new law is a compromise." He gave Broken Trail a keen look. "When you came here to tell me about the treatment of Chloe Cooley, you talked as though you were opposed to slavery."

"I am opposed to slavery."

"Then what are you doing working for a slave owner?"

Broken Trail felt his face turn red. This was a question he constantly asked himself. "Thayendanegea and I work together because we share one common goal. We both want to unite all the Native tribes in one federation. If we succeed, it will make us stronger in negotiating treaties with white governments."

"You say 'we' as if you were one of them."

"I am one of them. The Oneidas adopted me when I was ten years old. Captain Brant chose me to be his deputy because I know the ways of both worlds."

"Hmm. Very interesting. If you were ten when the Oneidas adopted you, you must have some memory of your original family."

"I remember my mother and father, my two brothers and my baby sister. Of course, Hope isn't a baby any longer. If she's alive, she's fourteen years old. I sometimes think about my white family, but I doubt I'll ever see any of them again."

"Well, stranger things have happened." Simcoe stood up. "It's going to take me a day or two to prepare an answer to Captain Brant's invitation. So I must arrange a suitable place for you to stay while you wait. As the representative of a great chief, a prince among the Six Nations, you're entitled to a respectful reception."

Broken Trail gave a slight bow. "Thank you, sir. Where shall I lodge?"

"A certain gentleman owes me a favour. His name is Andrew Steele. Come with me. I'll take you to his home. Mr. Steele has a profitable business that depends on my grace and favour. He supplies provisions for the Indian Department at Niagara." A faint smile passed over Simcoe's lips. "He won't be able to think of an excuse."

• • •

Mr. Steele's home was on a bluff overlooking the Niagara River, across from the ramparts and bastions of Fort Niagara on the United States side. Simcoe led the way.

"Before you meet Mr. Steele, you should know this—he's a slave owner. He hates the new law, but I put so much pressure on him that he had to vote for it. Slave owners don't talk about the new law when slaves are present. However, most slaves have heard rumours that changes are coming. They don't know what those changes are. Right now, everybody is jumpy."

"Thank you for the warning." Broken Trail groaned inwardly as he prepared himself for an uncomfortable visit.

They followed the flagstone path to the front door. Simcoe lifted the shiny brass knocker, which was shaped like a lion's head, and rapped firmly.

The man who opened the door was tall, broad-shouldered and solidly built. His skin was brown and his black hair touched with grey. He wore a short coat and breeches of dark red velvet. His snowy white shirt was ruffled at the front, and a frill of lace peaked from the cuff. Every detail of his livery advertised that his master was a wealthy man.

"Good evening, Joseph," Simcoe greeted him.

Joseph gave a warm smile. "Good evening, Governor." Then he raised his voice in a joyful shout. "Blow ye the trumpet, blow! The day of Jubilee is come!" The power of his voice made Broken Trail jump as if a trumpet had been blown in his ear.

"Hmm. Don't get too excited. Tomorrow is not yet here." Simcoe's voice dropped. "Not by a long way, alas."

Sobered by Simcoe's rebuke, Joseph asked, "Shall I fetch Mr. Steele?"

"Please do."

When Joseph had left them, Simcoe's face grew dark. "The new law won't free Joseph and his family. They don't know that yet."

"Why not tell them?"

Simcoe shook his head. "Even though I'm Lieutenant-Governor, I can't say anything until the new law is proclaimed. They will learn the truth tomorrow."

While they waited, the only sound was the ticking of the tall clock that stood in the hall. After a few moments, Mr. Steele appeared. He was a red-faced man, florid and plump, his belly straining the brocade of his dark blue waistcoat. Mr. Steele and the Lieutenant-Governor bowed to each other and, after an exchange of greetings, Simcoe introduced Broken Trail. "This young man is Captain Joseph Brant's deputy. I must impose on your hospitality to ask that you receive him as your guest for the next few days."

"Oh!" Mr. Steele looked momentarily shaken. "I'm delighted to oblige." He cast a sideways glance at Broken Trail, taking in his deerskin leggings and scalp lock. If he also noticed that his guest's eyes were blue, he showed no surprise. He turned to Joseph. "Tell Sukie to bring refreshments to the parlour."

The parlour, where Mr. Steele invited them to sit down, seemed dark after the brightness of the sunshine outside. A looking glass hung above the mantel and a carpet covered the floor in front of an unlit fireplace. Seated in an overstuffed chair, Broken Trail listened to the ticking of the hall clock while Simcoe and Mr. Steele exchanged pleasantries. After a few minutes, a black woman wearing a white apron over her plain brown dress silently entered carrying a bowl of rum punch, a plate of biscuits and three tumblers on a silver platter.

"That will be all, Sukie," Mr. Steele said when she had set down the platter. Broken Trail noticed the twitch of a smile on her lips as she left the room.

"Did you see that smile?" Mr. Steele poured the punch and passed the tumblers to his guests. "Our slaves listen at keyholes, and when they go to the market they spread rumours about what they think they heard."

"Slaves have ears, like the rest of us," Simcoe said calmly. "Of course, it would be better if their hopes had not been raised."

"Much better. The rumour that all the slaves will be freed tomorrow has made them insolent."

After raising his glass to his lips, Broken Trail set it untasted upon the table next to his chair. Having seen much harm done by strong drink, he avoided it completely.

"Tomorrow will be a difficult day." Simcoe's eyes were solemn. "Many will be heartbroken to learn that their dream of freedom will not come true. Others will be angry."

Broken Trail noticed how tightly Mr. Steele clutched his tumbler. His knuckles were white. *He'd like to throw it at Governor Simcoe*, Broken Trail thought. *But he doesn't dare, not when he wants to keep his profits from selling provisions to the Indian Department.*

The Lieutenant-Governor calmly sipped his drink. "I'm grateful for your support of my bill, Mr. Steele. Upper Canada will be the first jurisdiction in the entire British Empire to pass a law limiting slavery."

Mr. Steele's red face turned purple. "Perhaps," he sputtered, "we might find some other topic of conversation?" But after a few attempts, during which the hall clock ticked loudly, no agreeable topic could be found. Simcoe rose to take his leave.

After escorting Simcoe to the door, Mr. Steele returned to the parlour and poured himself another glass. "It's a messy business. Simcoe has great plans, but he's blind to reality. He states over and over that we need to increase our population. But, thanks to his new law, immigrants won't be able to bring their slaves with them. The very minute a slave crosses the border into Upper Canada, he'll be free. As a result, the better class of people will go to Nova Scotia, New Brunswick and Lower Canada, where they can keep their slaves."

*Better class of people? Slave owners?* Broken Trail reminded himself that he was a warrior, trained not to let his face reveal his feelings. He was also a guest in this man's home.

Mr. Steele continued. "Do you know what most of us will do? We'll find buyers outside the province and sell our slaves before the price collapses." He emptied his glass before going on. "Under this new law, any baby born to a slave becomes free at the age of twenty-five. So what's the point of feeding, clothing and training a young one who's going to walk away free just when he or she becomes most valuable? It isn't worth the expense." He stood up with a grunt. "The light's fading. I'll show you to your room before we need a candle."

Broken Trail picked up his carrying basket and rifle and followed Mr. Steele from the parlour and up a flight of stairs. The room to which Mr. Steele led him had a high bed with heavy curtains. The air felt stuffy and smelled stale. The single window was closed.

"You can find your way to the kitchen in the morning. Sukie will give you breakfast. I prefer a tray in my room, where I can look over business papers before leaving for my warehouse."

Although Broken Trail sensed an insult in being sent to the kitchen for his breakfast, he was glad that he would not be joining his host. As soon as Mr. Steele left him, he flung open the window and welcomed the fresh breeze and a robin's evening song. Looking out the window, he saw in the yard behind the house a small stable, a vegetable garden and a wooden hut. Standing in the open doorway of the hut was

Sukie, her arm around a skinny black girl, about twelve years old. The girl's white, homespun gown was too short, barely covering her knees. In this outgrown garment, she looked mostly arms and legs.

Below him, Broken Trail heard the back door open and close. There was Joseph, still wearing his livery. He crossed the yard in the shadowy darkness and joined the girl and Sukie. The three stood on the doorstep of the hut, watching the moon rise.

It lifted itself big and round into the sky, bathing the yard in silvery light. *Mother Moon*, Broken Trail said to himself. He felt its magic, knowing that this same moon was shining over the longhouses of the faraway village where his Oneida family had long been awaiting his return. Perhaps the same moon shone over his white family, wherever they were, and he felt a quiet joy that the moon shone for people of every nation.

He stayed at the window and watched until Joseph, Sukie and the girl entered the hut. The girl went in first, then Joseph with his arm across Sukie's shoulders. The door of the hut closed.

Broken Trail turned away from the window. There was not enough light for him to unpack his carrying basket. He pulled his knife and tomahawk from his belt, undressed and climbed into bed. He did not pull the bed curtains. Downstairs, the hall clock sounded ten, half-past-ten, eleven. He lay awake wondering what the next day would bring.

CHAPTER 3

# Proclamation Day

❧

In the morning, the delicious smell of baking bread led Broken Trail to a bright kitchen with white-washed walls. There was a cooking fireplace with a pull-out crane that held a variety of kettles. Hams hung on hooks from the ceiling beams. At a wooden table sat Joseph, Sukie and the girl Broken Trail had seen with them at the door of the hut. All three were eating, and they raised their faces when he entered the kitchen. They looked hard at him. The girl studied his scalp lock.

"Did Master send you to eat with us?" Sukie asked.

"Yes, ma'am." He bowed. The girl tittered to see him offer this courtesy.

"That will do, Rosa," Sukie rebuked her. "When we're free, we'll get used to white people showing respect, though I'm not sure this young fellow counts as white."

"I was born white, but raised Indian. I count myself lucky to be both."

"Anything's luckier than being black." Sukie got up to set a place for him.

"Now, Sukie," Joseph objected. "By the end of this day, you and me and Rosa are going to be just as free as Mr. Steele himself." A smile spread across his face. "Hallelujah!"

There was nothing Broken Trail could say, knowing what terrible disappointment lay in store for them. He sat down at the table and tucked into the ham and eggs that Sukie set before him.

"What's your name?" Rosa asked. "Do you have an Indian name and a white name?"

"I have two names. Broken Trail and Moses."

"We'll call you Moses," said Joseph. "The Bible tells us that Moses led the Hebrew people out of slavery in the Land of Egypt. It is surely a sign of God's grace that somebody with that name is here with us on this day."

Broken Trail felt uncomfortable at being likened to Moses in the Bible, but before he could protest, Rosa gave a happy shout. "Freedom! No more fireplaces to clean! No more chamber pots to empty. I can do as I please all day long."

"No, you can't," Joseph chided. "We'll still do our work. I'll wait the table and tend the horses. Mama will cook and do the laundry. You'll make beds and empty the chamber pots—"

"Not me!" Rosa jumped to her feet, knocking her chair over backwards.

"Rosa, don't interrupt your Daddy!" Sukie scolded.

"Well, I won't empty chamber pots after I'm free." She righted her chair and sat down again, scowling.

Joseph ignored the interruption. "The difference is this— from now on, Master will have to pay us. If he won't, then we'll go work for somebody who will."

Broken Trail kept his eyes on his plate. He knew the truth—Joseph, Sukie and Rosa would learn it soon enough. The clock was striking ten when he finished his breakfast. He turned to Sukie as he rose from the table. "Thank you kindly."

"Join us anytime," said Joseph. "Unless Mr. Steele expects you to dine with him."

"I don't know what Mr. Steele expects."

Outside the kitchen, the house seemed empty. The only sound was the ticking of the clock in the front hall. Mr. Steele must have gone to his warehouse. This was a busy day for others, but not for Broken Trail. How should he spend the empty hours that stretched before him?

Of course! He would go into town. Today was Proclamation Day. Crowds would be gathering. This was something he should see for himself.

He returned to his room. At the looking glass, he checked his appearance. His scalp lock looked greasy from the bear fat he used to keep it standing up. His blue eyes reminded him that he was not, and never could be, completely the warrior that he wanted to be. He scowled at his reflection. He wasn't exactly white, and he wasn't exactly Oneida. What was he, then? Joseph wanted to call him Moses. Could he live up to such a name? He knew the Bible story. As a small boy, he had been taken to church every Sunday by his white parents. Broken Trail hated slavery. Could he, like Moses, deliver slaves from bondage?

When he went outside, he stood blinking, his hand shading his eyes. He should have been able to see more clearly, coming out of darkness, yet he felt almost blinded by the light.

• • •

The town of Newark was milling with people of all sorts—soldiers, farmers, traders and warriors of several nations. Wagons and ox carts jammed the streets. The air was thick with the smell of animals and all kinds of waste. People on foot were all hurrying in the same direction. In front of a building near the riverbank, a crowd was gathering. The sign over the building's entrance read *Masonic Hall*. There were about fifty white men and a scattering of white women in the crowd, but not one black person. Broken Trail pushed his way to the front.

After a few minutes, the door opened and a man emerged.

He wore a red-and-gold coat, white breeches, black boots and a black tricorne hat, and he carried a large brass handbell. Following him was a soldier who held, in both hands, a long sheet of paper. The man in the colourful uniform glared about on all sides. Then he rang the bell. He rang it and rang it with such a tremendous clang that many in the crowd covered their ears. When there was no doubt that he had everybody's attention, he gave the bell to the soldier and took from him the sheet of paper. After taking a breath so deep that his chest swelled and his face turned red, he began his proclamation.

"Oyez, oyez oyez! Whereas it is unjust that a people who enjoy Freedom by Law should encourage the introduction of Slavery in this Province, and whereas it is highly expedient to abolish Slavery in the Province so far as the same may gradually be done without violating private property; Be it enacted . . ."

He took in a deep breath, expelled it, and continued for the next quarter of an hour before finishing with a triumphant shout: "God Save the King!"

There were some cheers, but just as many curses. Then the soldier handed him a hammer and a nail with which he posted the paper on the front door of the building.

The crowd dispersed. As Broken Trail walked away, his thoughts turned to Joseph, Sukie and Rosa. The new law enacted exactly what Lieutenant-Governor Simcoe had told him it would. It wouldn't take long for the news to reach them. By the next time he saw them, they would know the truth. What should he say to them then?

Absorbed in these thoughts, Broken Trail barely noticed the girl who was walking toward him with a large, black-and-white, shaggy dog at her side. She did not attract his full attention until she was so close that they nearly collided.

CHAPTER 4

# A Girl Named Hope

❧

"Excuse me."

He stepped out of the way. As he did so, he took a look at the girl. It was not her white ruffled cap that he noticed, nor her homespun dress, nor the basket that hung from the crook of her elbow. What he saw was his white mother's face. Blue eyes. Turned-up nose. But it was not Ma's face as he last saw it, sallow and creased with worry lines. The girl's face was smooth with rosy skin. He remembered a miniature of his mother, painted when she was young, that she wore in a silver locket around her neck. That miniature could have been a portrait of this girl. The sight of her took his breath away, and he felt for a moment as if his heart had stopped beating. A ghost! But no. The girl was alive.

Her blue eyes opened wide. In an instant, she quickly glanced away, as any girl would do upon finding herself eye-to-eye with a young man she did not know. Then she quickened her step and kept on going.

Should he follow? If he caught up with the girl, what would he say? *"Excuse me, but you look like my mother?"* He could not imagine how she might respond.

But something about his appearance had startled her. Maybe it was just his scalp lock. Or could it be more? A family resemblance? Broken Trail had blue eyes and a snub nose like his brother, Elijah. If the girl was his sister, Hope, did she know that she had another brother who had been missing for years? If she did, could she have wondered whether she would ever meet him? If Hope was alive, she would be about the same age as this girl. What a fool he would look if he followed her, asked who she was, and it turned out that she was not his sister! But what did he risk? Nothing worse than a moment's embarrassment if he said, *"Are you Hope Cobman?"* and she answered, *"No,"* leaving him to apologize and never see her again. So he would take the chance. Even while thinking these thoughts, he lost sight of the girl, for she stood only shoulder-high to the men who were all around her. If he didn't catch up, he might lose track of her completely. He started moving, slowly at first, then faster, pushing his way through the mass of people. By the time he reached the river road, he was in the clear. There, ahead of him, he saw the girl and the dog.

He slowed his pace. No need to hurry. It was enough to keep her in sight. He needed time to think of what he would say when he spoke to her. Between him and the girl were a man and woman on foot and a slow-moving wagon drawn by a pair of oxen, piled high with sawn lumber.

After a time, the couple on foot turned off the road. Now there was only the wagon between Broken Trail and the girl.

He had been following her for about five miles when she and the dog turned north onto a footpath toward a log cabin. At the start of the path, he saw a sign nailed to the trunk of a tree: H. COBMAN. His heart beat fast. So he was right!

The time had come for him to act. He did not want to frighten her, for he knew that any girl would be frightened to suddenly become aware of a man coming behind her. The path was shadowed by trees. He must let her know that she was in no danger from him.

He waited until the wagon went by. Then, standing in the middle of the road so that she could see him, he shouted, "Hello, there! You, with the dog! I want to talk to you."

She spun around. As soon as she saw him, she shifted her basket so that she was holding it with both hands in front of her like a shield. At the same instant, the dog thrust itself between them, snarling, teeth bared. Broken Trail saw its yellow eyes. Wolf-dog.

"I'm sorry to frighten you." He took two steps up the path toward her.

"I'm not frightened." Her lower lip jutted defiantly. "You're the fellow who nearly bumped into me. What do you want?"

He had seen the way her eyes widened when she saw his face. Blood calls to blood. Didn't she know? Was she pretending not to know?

The dog's hackles were up. It kept on snarling, the slobber dripping from its fangs. For a moment, no words came to him. Then he said, simply, "You look like my mother."

A minute passed. The dog growled. Birds twittered in the trees. There was no other sound. The girl stared at his face, at his scalp lock. Their eyes met. "I look . . ." Her voice trembled, as if she hardly knew what she was saying or what it might mean. "I look like my mother."

"Who are you?"

"I don't give my name to strangers."

"I'll give you mine. Moses Cobman. That was my name as a child."

She stepped back, looking shaken, and glanced about as if needing somewhere to sit down. The dog growled ferociously, ready to lunge.

"Quiet, Captain." She spoke calmly. The dog stopped growling, lowered its head and grovelled away backward with an aggrieved whimper.

"Now tell me your name, since I have told you mine."

"Hope."

"Just Hope?"

"Hope Cobman."

"Then you know who I am."

"Yes. You are my brother." Her lips formed the words, but

he barely heard the sound. She lowered the basket so that, no longer held like a shield, it dangled from the crook of her elbow. For a time they stared at each other, neither speaking a word. When she finally broke the silence, her voice was unsteady. "I've waited a long time. You see, I knew I had one more brother to find. Ma told me I had three older brothers. Silas, Elijah and Moses."

*Silas. Elijah.* How long had it been since he'd heard anyone speak his brothers' names—his brothers' names that were also her brothers' names?

"So you found Silas and Elijah, if I'm the only brother you still had to find."

"Silas is dead, killed in battle." Hope's eyes lowered. "Elijah lives with the Cherokee Indians, far away in the Tennessee Mountains."

"Years ago, Elijah and I made a long trail through Cherokee lands."

"He was here in Niagara last summer, and then he went back. He's married to a Cherokee girl."

Broken Trail's mind whirled with so many questions that he did not know where to begin.

Hope must have sensed his confusion. "I knew I had a father and three brothers, but I didn't know where they were. So after Ma died, I wanted to find them."

"Ma died?" He caught his breath. "When did she die?"

"Two years ago. I'm sorry to tell you like this. Of course, you didn't know."

"I wondered sometimes how she was—if she was still alive.

It's been a long time since I last saw her. I was a child when the Oneidas carried me off."

"I was just a baby. Ma told me I was one month old when it happened."

"You were born in the forest after rebels torched our home. You had no name. I told Ma you had to have a name. So she named you Hope. I remember that day as clear as anything."

"Ma told me how Mohawk warriors took us in a big canoe to Carleton Island. I grew up in the barracks at Fort Haldimand. It's not far from Kingston, even though it's part of the United States now. After Ma died, I spent a year in an orphanage. Then I was indentured to look after an old lady. She died after just a few months. That's when I started searching for the rest of my family." Hope paused. "I learned that Pa had served in a regiment called Butler's Rangers, and that after the war Colonel Butler settled his Rangers along the Niagara River. I found Pa right here. This was his land. It's my land now. He left it to me. That's my home." She pointed to the log cabin. "We can talk there."

When they reached the door, she pressed the latch and waved him inside. She followed, leaving the door open. The dog came with them into the cabin. It circled three times before sinking with a groan to the floor, where it lay with its snout pointed at Broken Trail, its ears erect and its yellow eyes wide open.

The cabin was small, just one room. It had a narrow bed with a Hudson's Bay blanket as a cover. The only other furnishings were two battered chairs and a scuffed table. A fireplace took up most of the wall opposite the door. Two shelves were built into the wall on his left. On the lower shelf were plates, bowls, cups and tumblers. On the upper shelf were a Bible, writing materials, a stack of paper and a row of paint pots, one of them holding several small brushes.

Broken Trail saw that his sister had made a cozy home for herself, no different from other Loyalist homes he had visited. It was when he turned to face the wall on his right that he gasped, astonished, for hanging on the wall were three paintings, and one of them was a portrait of his mother. She looked straight at him from the frame.

"What! How did this—" he sputtered. "How?"

"I painted it. It's a copy of this miniature." She unfastened the clasp of a slender chain from around her neck, pulled a silver locket from the top of her bodice and handed it to him. When Broken Trail clicked it open, he recognized the tiny portrait that his mother had worn in that very locket so long ago. He looked from the miniature in his hand to the painting on the wall, and then at his sister. Same pastel prettiness. Same brown hair. Same turned-up nose.

"Wonderful," he marvelled.

She blushed. "It's just copying."

"It's more than that. You make her seem alive. It's like Ma's right here, looking at us." It was true. The face of the woman in the portrait had a softness that spoke of quiet joy.

"I feel that she is here, and that she knows." Hope's voice

shook a little. "I always believed that someday I'd find you—though, as it turns out, you have found me."

"Who taught you to paint? You must have a teacher." They stood side by side, looking at the picture.

"Nobody. A friend gave me paper and pencils when he saw that I like to draw. I make sketches in pencil. During last winter, there wasn't much for me to do. I had plenty of time to finish my sketches in watercolours."

Broken Trail glanced at the second painting. "I recognize this place. The bastions. The ramparts. It's Fort Niagara, from the Canadian side."

"I've painted other scenes of the fort. This is the one I like most."

"It's peaceful. You don't show the big guns, the cannons pointing across the river."

"I don't like to think about those."

Now they turned to the third painting. It was a picture of a black man running on a moonlit road. Over his shoulder he carried a bundle on a stick. Behind him a pine tree, bent by the wind, strained in the same direction as the man was running. The man's feet were bare. He ran with his head up, unafraid and determined.

"I've seen this figure before. But not like this. It isn't just a copy."

"It began as a copy. I'll show you." She walked across the room to the shelf that held the writing materials and rifled through the stack of papers until she found what she was looking for. It was a poster, torn at all four corners, offering a reward for the return of a slave.

"This was nailed to the door of the Masonic Lodge in Newark. I ripped it from the door." Hope handed him the poster.

The running figure was the same as the figure she had painted, but she had added movement and colour. Broken Trail read the poster's message silently:

### FIVE POUNDS REWARD

*Run-away from his Master at Kingston, a Negro Man named JUPITER about 27 years of age — 5 feet 8 inches high — and supposed to have come this way. Any person securing such Run-Away so that his Master can get him again, shall be entitled to the above Reward, by applying to the Printer hereof.*

*Queenston, May 5, 1793.*
*Jeremiah Smith*

After a moment, Broken Trail asked, "Did they catch him?"
She smiled. "Not so far as I know."
"You sound as though you're against slavery."
"I hate the idea that one person can own another. Being an indentured servant is almost as bad as being a slave. The old lady I took care of was mean to me. So I understand what it's like to be a slave."

"Would you help a runaway slave?"

"Indeed I would! I'd hide him in my cabin."

He looked around. The cabin's one and only room measured about ten feet by twelve feet. "Where could you hide anyone here?"

"I'd find a way."

"I reckon you would." He looked at that jutting lower lip and defiant chin. His sister. They had named her Hope when nobody really expected her to live. Look at her now! "You must know about the new law. Is that what took you to Newark today? Did you want to be there when it was proclaimed?" He studied the picture of the black man running on the moonlit road.

"Of course I wanted to be there. But I was going into town anyway. I supply fresh eggs to the Officers' Mess at Navy Hall. That's how I earn my living. In the chicken coop behind my cabin, I keep twenty laying hens and a rooster. Well, I was on my way to Navy Hall to deliver eggs, when I saw a crowd gathered around the steps of the Masonic Hall. There stood the town crier clanging a bell and shouting 'Oyez, oyez!' I stopped to listen. He started reading a great long paper. Men standing all around me were arguing and shaking their fists. I left quickly. Since I carried two dozen eggs in my basket, I didn't want to be caught in a riot."

"There was no riot. You and I must have arrived about the same time, but I didn't see you in the crowd. Did you hear anything the man said?"

"He shouted 'whereas' a couple of times. I stayed long enough to hear him say that it was a good idea to abolish slavery as long as it didn't interfere with private property."

"Yes, that's it." Broken Trail sighed. "Slaves are private property. That's why the new law doesn't free any slaves in this province. Yet slaves coming here are free the minute they cross the border."

"If that's what it means, it isn't fair."

"You're right. It's not fair." His mind turned to Joseph, Sukie and Rosa. By now, they must have known that they would never be free. How bitter and heartbroken they must feel!

"What's wrong?" asked Hope. "You look upset. Is it something I said?"

"Sorry. It's nothing you said. I just thought about three fine, decent people who learned today that they're going to be slaves for life. They're a family—father, mother and a girl not much younger than you. Their owner is a man named Andrew Steele. I'm staying at his house in Newark for a few days. Hope, I must help them."

"Of course you must."

"They must be feeling desperate. It would help for me to go to them and tell them that they can count on me."

"It would help. And Moses, let me know if I can help."

"I will." He looked down at his sister's intent, serious face, and their eyes met. "You and I have many stories to share. I'll return as soon as I can." He took a step toward the door.

"Wait! I'll make you a cup of tea before you go."

"Next time. Then we'll sit and drink tea and talk for hours. We'll get to know each other."

"We've made a good start already. We know we both hate slavery. We both want to help enslaved people."

Suddenly, without knowing he was going to do it, he turned back and seized her hands. "Goodbye for now, little sister."

"Just a minute, there's one more thing. Pa left money. He hid it under the floor. When I found it, I thought, *This isn't just for me.* I spent some to buy chickens. The rest is still there—for our brother Elijah, if I see him. And for you."

"Money? Not for me. It's yours, not mine. Anyway, I have little need for money."

"I can't keep it all. Your share will be waiting for you if you ever need it."

"Thank you. I'll remember that."

Seeing him about to leave, the dog lifted its head and heaved itself from its resting place on the floor. Hope waved to Broken Trail from the doorstep, but the dog followed him along the path all the way to the road, growling softly to make certain that he would go away.

# CHAPTER 5

# A Turn in the Trail

He started back to Newark at the jogging pace that a warrior used on a long trail. It was a pace that let him run all day without tiring but left the mind free. As he jogged, he retraced in his mind every moment from his first sight of Hope until his last glimpse of her waving goodbye. He felt overwhelmed by the fact that he had found his sister. Well, not exactly found her. Bumped into her was closer to the truth. Even so, it didn't feel like an accident. Many times over the years, he had sensed the Invisible Spirits guiding him. They had a plan for his life. Bringing him and Hope together must be part of that plan. It wasn't a coincidence that it happened on Proclamation Day. He was ready to fight against slavery, and so was she. It was a sign that brother and sister were meant to join forces in this fight.

Yesterday he hadn't even known she was still alive. This morning, when he saw her in Newark, the shock of recognition had taken his breath away. From the way her eyes widened, he knew that she felt the same. Brother and sister. Born to the same parents. Sharing the same blood.

At first, as he jogged along the river road, his thoughts were about his sister and the partnership they would form. As the distance to Newark grew shorter, he began to think about the problems he would face. The biggest problem was his link with Thayendanegea. Whenever Broken Trail stayed in his home at Brant's Ford, slaves waited on him. Thayendanegea knew he hated slavery. To keep relations smooth between them, he had given up rebuking Broken Trail for thanking Sophia every time she refilled his plate or his water glass. Thanking Sophia seemed to please her, and it made him feel better. But it didn't change the fact that accepting her services made him part of the system. This was wrong.

He had spoken with Sophia the morning he left Brant's Ford to carry Thayendanegea's invitation to the Lieutenant-Governor. She was washing dishes when he went into the kitchen to say goodbye. "Sophia," he'd said, "I'll be away for a few days. Thayendanegea is sending me to Niagara with a message for the new Lieutenant-Governor."

"You take orders from Thayendanegea just like me. Is he

your master?" She'd lifted a plate from the sudsy water and set it on a cloth that was spread for dishes to dry.

"No." He had hesitated. "I mean, yes, I suppose he is. I do what he tells me to do."

"Could he sell you?"

"Uh, no. It doesn't work like that."

"I think Master plans to sell me. He told me I was worth one hundred dollars, New York money." There had been pride in her voice as she shared this information.

"One hundred dollars is a lot of money." A first-rate horse cost thirty dollars, but Broken Trail wasn't sure he ought to tell her this. Sophia might not appreciate her value being compared with that of a horse.

"If I had one hundred dollars," she'd asked, "do you suppose I could buy myself?"

"Maybe you could. I've heard about a slave owner who let his slave do odd jobs for neighbours so long as he had his own work done. The slave saved up the pay he earned until he had enough to buy his freedom."

"So it can happen." She'd sighed. "But only for lucky folks who have a master like that."

"You're right." Then he'd cast diplomacy aside. "The kindness of a few does not justify a system that is evil."

"Evil! My word! What would Captain Brant say if he heard you talk like that?"

This was the very question Broken Trail was asking himself when he reached Mr. Steele's home. He rapped on the door. When no one came, he pressed the latch and entered. The hall clock struck four as if it had been awaiting his arrival. After its gong had died away, he heard nothing but tick-tock, tick-tock. He was halfway to the kitchen when Joseph's rumbling voice reached him.

"God told Abraham his descendants would be slaves in a land that was not theirs and their affliction would last for four hundred years." His solemn tone did not change when Broken Trail appeared at the open doorway. "Who are we to expect the Lord to set us free after a time not half so long? The day of Jubilee will come. Just not yet. While we wait, God expects us to obey our owner's commands. It says in the Good Book, 'Slaves, obey your masters.'"

Joseph was sitting on one side of the table facing his wife and daughter, neither of whom looked as resigned as Joseph to their fate.

"I don't want to wait," Sukie said. "I thought the new law was going to free us, but it doesn't do us one bit of good. You and me and Rosa will be slaves the rest of our lives. I don't care that babies born from this day forward will be free when they turn twenty-five. All I ask is that someday, our little Rosa will be free." Sukie patted the girl's hand.

"That's not going to happen. So we must make the best of it and thank the Lord for the blessings of this life."

Rosa lifted her head. "Not me! I'm not going to thank the Lord for leaving me here to empty Master's chamber pot for the rest of my life."

"Hush, now!" Sukie had just noticed Broken Trail standing in the doorway.

He entered the kitchen and stood at one end of the table, where he could see all their faces. Joseph's was dignified, Sukie's was indignant and Rosa's angry features were bunched up in a scowl.

"I'm sorry," he told them. "Lieutenant-Governor Simcoe did the best he could."

"Master can empty his own chamber pot," Rosa muttered.

"Girl, don't you talk like that, else he might sell you across the border and you'll end up picking cotton down south, where the master will abuse you and the overseer will beat you, and you'll be locked up every night." As Sukie was speaking, Broken Trail heard the sound of heavy shoes approaching along the hall.

"Hush!" Joseph warned. All were silent when Mr. Steele entered the kitchen. He fixed Rosa, Sukie and Joseph each in turn with a cold stare.

"Get on with your work." He spoke with menacing slowness. Then he turned to Broken Trail. "You will dine with me this evening. Eight o'clock." And he was gone.

Broken Trail went to the kitchen door, closed it firmly and turned to face the others. "Don't give up! There are some places in the world that have ended slavery. Someday, it will happen here."

"Where are those places?" Joseph asked.

"England is one. Some of the United States are making it

illegal. In Vermont, where I went to school, every male slave must be freed at age twenty-one and every female at age eighteen."

"What about children?" Rosa asked.

"I wondered about that," Broken Trail answered. "It sounds strange, doesn't it? Maybe they think children have no rights."

"So if we lived in Vermont Mama and Daddy would be free, but I'd be a slave for another six years. That's not fair."

"Certainly not fair, but better than 'slave for life,' the way it is here. Vermont's not the only state that's passed laws against slavery. There's Pennsylvania, New Hampshire, Massachusetts and a couple of others."

Sukie raised her eyebrows. "Maybe we should run away and escape to one of those places."

Broken Trail shook his head. "Even in the free states, there are slave catchers that make their living rounding up fugitive slaves. You'd likely be caught, sent back and punished. We must find a way to make you legally free."

"How?" Sukie asked.

"That's what I'm going to find out. I'll ask Governor Simcoe. He might know of a way."

"Hmm. While I wait, I'd better get on with making dinner." Sukie gave Broken Trail a tiny smile. "It has to be something extra good, because you're going to dine with Mr. Steele tonight."

"I'd rather eat here in the kitchen with you. But maybe while we're eating, he'll say something that can help me make a plan."

# CHAPTER 6

# A Business Proposition

On the dining room table, Sukie had set out a platter of roast beef, bowls of potatoes and other vegetables and a plate of warm rolls. There was red wine in a crystal decanter. Two places were set with fine china, wine glasses and gleaming silver. From the ceiling, a chandelier with ten candles flooded the room with light. Broken Trail was impressed. Not even at Thayendanegea's home had he witnessed such splendour.

Joseph waited table, attired in his dark red velvet breeches and jacket and white ruffled shirt. As he passed the dishes, his face remained completely expressionless. For one brief moment his eyes met Broken Trail's, and then Joseph turned his head away.

When Joseph approached to fill the wine glasses, Broken Trail placed his hand over his glass. Seeing this, Mr. Steele raised his eyebrows in surprise. "Don't you drink wine? I expected you to indulge. Living as you do, among the Native people, I thought you would share their habits. But that's all right. Sobriety gives you an advantage."

"That's what I think, too," said Broken Trail, though he had no idea what Mr. Steele had in mind.

"You may wonder why I asked you to dine with me."

"I thought it must be out of courtesy to Lieutenant-Governor Simcoe, since he asked you to receive me as your guest."

"That's true. I do have the obligations of a host. But I am also a man of business." He leaned toward Broken Trail. "I have, in my warehouse, a shipload of rum from the West Indies. It's worth thousands of pounds. There's a fortune to be made if I can find the right customer."

"Surely you don't mean me!"

"As a customer, you aren't worth a penny. But as my agent, you're just what I'm looking for."

"As your agent?"

"You're Joseph Brant's deputy, aren't you?"

"Yes."

"That gives you great influence among the Six Nations people living along the Grand River. I've heard there are villages all the way from the mouth of the river up to Brant's Ford."

"That's true. There are villages of the Onondagas, Senecas, Tuscaroras and Oneidas, in that order, with the Mohawks at Brant's Ford the furthest up the river."

"How many people does that add up to?"

"Maybe four thousand. The number keeps growing as more and more refugees come from the camp at Buffalo Creek. There are hundreds of homeless people at Buffalo Creek. They had their lands stolen from them."

"So we'll say four thousand. Let's suppose that each person drinks one gallon of rum every year. That's a conservative estimate."

Broken Trail felt his cheeks grow hot. "I catch your drift, and I don't like it. I've seen the harm that strong drink can do."

"I'm not asking you to drink it. Just help me sell it. You must know the name of every chief in every Indian village along the Grand River. What would it take to get a chief working for us in every village? One hundred pounds apiece? A share of the profit? Maybe an unlimited supply of rum for his own consumption."

Broken Trail, trembling with fury, set down his knife and fork. He wanted to push back his chair from the table and walk out of the room. But he must not do that. Not while he was a guest in this man's house, introduced by Upper Canada's Lieutenant-Governor. To restrain himself took all of his training as a diplomat.

"Sir, I cannot be a partner in such a business."

"I haven't told you what I'm prepared to pay."

"That doesn't matter. If you offered me King George's Royal Treasury, I'd still say no."

There was the twitch of a smile on Joseph's lips as he stepped forward to refill Mr. Steele's wine glass.

"Think it over. Think of the things that money can buy." With a flourish of his hand, Mr. Steele flaunted the luxuries on his table and all the rich furnishings of the room. "Imagine what you could do with a thousand pounds."

This was something Broken Trail could easily imagine. Sophia Pooley, Joseph, Sukie, Rosa. If he had one thousand pounds, he could buy all four to set them free. But that would not help the thousands of others who would remain enslaved. For him to buy and set free four slaves—or even ten times that number—would do nothing to end slavery. And so his answer would still be no.

Mr. Steele changed the subject. "I trust you are enjoying your dinner."

"It is excellent."

"Sukie's a tolerable cook. Keeping three slaves is an extravagance, seeing that I'm a single man. But I like to live in style. Besides that, I need to entertain people who are important for business. Even though the new legislation is going to make things difficult for slave owners in the future, the slaves I own are slaves for life. So everything in my household will go on as before. I can't complain."

# CHAPTER 7

# The Accident

❦

The next morning, a bang as sharp as a gunshot woke Broken Trail from sleep. In an instant he sprung out of bed and crouched, knife in hand, ready to fight. Even in a place as safe as Mr. Steele's guest room, he kept his knife handy under his pillow while he slept.

But there was no enemy here. Broken Trail heard a scurry of footsteps along the hall outside his room and then down the stairs. He relaxed and put his knife into its sheath, which lay attached to his belt on the chair beside his bed.

The sun was shining outside his open window. He must have overslept. That was easy to do when snuggled into a feather mattress. After he had washed, dressed and tidied his scalp lock, he went downstairs to the kitchen. Sukie and Rosa were there, but not Joseph.

"Good morning!" said Sukie, who was kneading a lump of bread dough on a floured board. Rosa, hunched at the table over a heap of silver tableware, was rubbing a silver spoon with a dark grey paste. She did not speak or raise her head.

"Good morning. Sukie, that was a delicious dinner last night. But sadly, my conversation with Mr. Steele didn't help me make a plan. All I learned is that he takes for granted that everything will go on just as before."

"That's what I expected."

"We can't give up! This morning I'm going to call on Governor Simcoe to ask for help. There must be some way we can free your family."

"Thank you, Moses. I pray there is. But Joseph is right when he says a loving family is more important than freedom."

"I reckon that's so, but free together is better than enslaved together." Broken Trail looked around. "Where is Joseph?"

"He's out in the stable rubbing down Mr. Steele's horse. Master's just come back from some business at Navy Hall."

Mr. Steele's heavy tread was audible as he ascended the stairs. Broken Trail heard his footsteps overhead as he went to his bedroom. Across the table, the silver spoon that Rosa was polishing shook in her hand.

Suddenly, a shout came from above. "Good God! What the devil!" A door slammed.

Sukie looked up from the kneading board. Rosa's head was bowed so low that Broken Trail could not see her face. Her shoulders heaved. The little cornrow bunches in which her hair was braided bobbed up and down.

Mr. Steele's footsteps clambered down the stairs and came closer. He burst into the kitchen. "This is an outrage! Where is that girl?" Then he saw Rosa cowering at the table. "Is this how you carry out your duties? My bedroom a pigsty! My Turkish carpet ruined!"

Sukie's face looked ashen. "Rosa, what happened?"

"I was carrying the chamber pot," she blubbered. "It slipped. It hit the fireplace fender." Her voice choked. "It broke."

Broken Trail could picture the scene—a full chamber pot smashing against the brass fireplace fender that surrounded the hearth, splashing the pot's contents all over the floor.

"Rosa, why did you lie?" Sukie lifted her hands from the lump of dough. "When I asked you about the crash I heard, you said it was the fire tongs hitting the fender."

"I was scared to tell you."

"But you could have gone right away with a bucket of water, a pail and a brush to clean up the mess before Master discovered it."

"I'm sorry," Rosa whimpered, starting to sob.

Sukie turned to Mr. Steele. "Rosa will clean it up. When she's done, there won't be a trace—"

At that moment, Joseph appeared in the doorway. "What's wrong?"

"Rosa had an accident carrying a chamber pot." Sukie

rested a hand on Rosa's shoulder. "She'll clean it up. Everything will be just fine."

"Nothing will be fine until the girl has been punished." Mr. Steele's tone was cold as ice. "Joseph, get my buggy whip from the stable."

"Oh, no!" Sukie moaned.

Joseph shook his head. "No, sir."

Broken Trail stepped forward. "Sir, it was an accident. Such punishment is not deserved."

Mr. Steele glared at him. "It's not your carpet that's been ruined. These are not your slaves."

"But the girl has said she's sorry. I think you should leave it at that."

"What you think has no bearing on this matter." Mr. Steele pointed his stubby finger at Joseph. "You heard me. Fetch the buggy whip!"

"No."

Mr. Steele's face grew red. "The girl must be punished. If we were back in Virginia, I'd send her to the House of Correction for a beating. But you can do it for me. Isn't it a father's duty to correct his child? Joseph, you quote the Bible every chance you get. You know what it says: 'Spare the rod and spoil the child.'"

"I know what the Bible says, but I'm not going to beat my little girl with a buggy whip. It's for horses, not for a child."

"You will do it, and you will do it now. Twenty strokes on her bare back. Get the whip."

"I will not."

Mr. Steele's eyes bulged with rage. "You are a slave. How dare you disobey my lawful command!"

"I am a slave, but I am also a man and a father." He took a step toward Mr. Steele, his eyes narrowed. Rosa stopped crying. She raised her head and looked from her father to her master. Nobody moved.

Suddenly, Sukie threw herself to her knees in front of Mr. Steele, her hands clasped together and her arms raised imploringly. "Please, Master. It was an accident. She's clumsy. Girls that age grow so fast. She doesn't deserve—"

Mr. Steele struck the side of her head with the flat of his hand, his lips parted in a cruel sneer.

With a roar, Joseph lunged at Mr. Steele. As he lunged, Broken Trail threw himself between them and took the force of Joseph's charge. Then he spun about and gave Joseph's chest a shove.

"No! Don't strike him! I'll take care of this!"

Joseph stepped back, chest heaving. His arms hung at his sides, but his fists were clenched.

Mr. Steele glared at him. "You're a slave. That's all you are." Then he turned to Sukie. "Make up a different room for me until I can use my own again."

He strutted out of the kitchen, chest puffed in pompous pride.

# CHAPTER 8
# Family Life, Enslaved

⟋⟍

"What can we do now?" Sukie asked.

Joseph steadied himself with both hands flat down on the table and his legs planted apart. "I don't know."

"I'm going to call on Governor Simcoe this morning." Broken Trail offered Sukie his hand and helped her up. "I'll tell him about this."

"You should wait." She sat down on a chair, her hand pressed to the side of her head where Mr. Steele had struck her.

"Why wait?" Broken Trail asked.

"Let things simmer down. When Mr. Steele thinks about

it, he'll realize it was an accident. No slave would do such a thing on purpose. Give him time to dust off his pride. What you need to do right now is apologize for not minding your own business."

"I refuse to apologize."

Joseph straightened up and turned around to face Broken Trail. "Thank you for stepping in. If I'd struck my master instead of striking you, we'd be in worse trouble than we are. Sukie's right. You should apologize to Mr. Steele. If you report this to Governor Simcoe, Master will be even angrier than he is right now."

"I don't think he'll accept my apology."

"It's worth a try," Sukie sighed. "Unless he throws you out of the house, act as though nothing happened. He was expecting you to have dinner with him this evening."

"Are you asking me to sit down to dinner with that man?"

"Yes, if he still wants you at his table."

"Very well. I'll apologize." *That's what Thayendanegea would tell me to do*, Broken Trail told himself. *He trained me in diplomacy to be prepared for times like this.*

• • •

Mr. Steele gritted his teeth as he listened to Broken Trail apologize for interfering in his domestic arrangements. But he accepted it. And so it was that Broken Trail dined again with Mr. Steele. This time, the overhead chandelier remained unlit. The wavering flames of two candles in candlesticks provided the only light. The food was just as plentiful as the previous evening, although Joseph was not there to serve it. Broken Trail wondered where he was.

Mr. Steele noticed him glancing around. "We have to serve ourselves. I've relieved Joseph of his duties."

"I hope he'll return to them soon. Joseph is an excellent servant."

Mr. Steele glowered. "How I deal with my slaves is my business, not yours. I think we've settled that point."

Silenced by this rebuke, Broken Trail took a slice of ham from a platter. He forced himself to eat, but each mouthful stuck in his throat.

Mr. Steele poured himself a glass of wine. "I'm selling Rosa and Joseph."

Broken Trail's fists tightened around his knife and fork.

"The girl isn't worth much," Mr. Steele continued. "She'll never be any use as a house servant. Field work is all she's good for. A jobber who deals in slaves happens to be in town. He buys them for auction in the United States. I saw him this afternoon. It's all settled. He'll give me forty dollars for an untrained female." He paused to butter a dinner roll. "Joseph's another matter. He's a good boy."

"Boy? How can you call a man close to forty years old a boy?" Broken Trail asked through clenched teeth.

"They're all boys—those black fellows. They ought to re-member it. In the Southern States, they have slave-whipping businesses with special equipment to deal with problems like disobedience. We need a service like that in Upper Canada. But since there are only five or six hundred slaves in the entire province, nobody could make money operating such a business." He dabbed his lips with his table napkin. "I can get a good price for Joseph—butler, valet, groom, wood chopper—he does it all. The jobber has offered one hundred and fifty dollars New York money for him. I'll take it. But I'll keep Sukie. She's a good cook and laundress. Now she can do the cleaning, too." He paused to drain his wine glass. "I'll hire a white man for the outdoor work. Plenty of disbanded soldiers are looking for employment."

"You can't do that!" Broken Trail dropped his cutlery to his plate.

"Do what?"

"Sell the father and the daughter but keep the mother here. They're a family!"

Mr. Steele laughed. "Family? Slaves don't have families. They're livestock. If Farmer Brown owns a bull, a cow and a calf, you don't say he owns a family of cattle."

"No, but—"

"If Farmer Brown owns a ram, a ewe and a lamb, do you address them as Mr. and Mrs. Sheep and family?"

"But—"

Mr. Steele was enjoying this. "If he has a boar, a sow and a little piglet, do you—"

Broken Trail jumped up, knocking over his chair. "Excuse me. I've lost my appetite."

. . .

Ten minutes later, back in his room, Broken Trail wished that
he had not knocked over the chair or slammed the dining
room door. As a warrior, he should hide his feelings. As a
diplomat, he should always behave in a courteous manner.

What should he do now? Even though it was getting dark,
he could still pack his carrying basket and leave. But he
couldn't rush out without telling Sukie and Joseph what had
happened. Sukie would still be in the kitchen, washing dinner dishes. Where was Joseph?

Just as importantly, he must visit the Lieutenant-Governor to explain his breach of diplomacy. When he described
how Mr. Steele talked about slaves as if they were animals,
Simcoe would pardon his outburst. But he couldn't impose
upon Simcoe at this late hour. Like it or not, he had to stay
here for one more night.

Broken Trail struggled with his thoughts as he packed his
carrying basket. When that was done, he went to the window
and looked out. The slave hut door was closed. By the light of
the moon, he saw a padlock glisten above the handle.

. . .

In the morning, Broken Trail rose early. When he had washed
and dressed, he picked up his rifle, hoisted his carrying basket onto his back and left the room, closing the door behind
him. The hall clock chimed eight as he entered the kitchen.
There was Sukie, chopping onions with a big knife. At first,

Broken Trail thought that she was alone. Then he saw a white man sitting in a chair against the wall. He was holding a wooden cudgel—not brandishing it, but resting it across his knees. He stared at Broken Trail with glaring eyes under heavy brows.

"Sukie!" Broken Trail called. She raised her head. Her appearance startled him, for he would not have thought that black skin could change to such a pallid grey. Her eyes were filled with grief and fear. When she saw him, her expression changed to one of desperate appeal. "Where are Joseph and Rosa?" he asked softly.

Her voice quavered. "In the middle of the night, men from the warehouse—" Her eyes flicked toward the man on the chair. "Men from the warehouse took them away."

The man rose, glaring at Broken Trail. He was squat in build, with a barrel chest and thick neck. "You, go away! This is none of your business."

Broken Trail fixed the man with an even fiercer glare. "I'm making it my business, and I'm not leaving until I've finished talking with Sukie." The man raised his cudgel. Broken Trail's fingers closed around the handle of the tomahawk in his belt. "I am Mr. Steele's guest. Remember that."

The man looked confused. He opened his mouth, but said nothing. Then he sank back onto his chair and tapped his fingers on the cudgel. He looked anxiously toward the door, perhaps hoping for Mr. Steele to appear and take charge.

Broken Trail ignored him and turned to Sukie. "Mr. Steele has no intention of selling you. He wants to keep you as a house slave. But he's going to sell Rosa and Joseph."

"I know. He told me that he's selling them to a jobber who'll take them to an auction in the United States."

"We can't let him do that. I'm going to see Governor Simcoe to ask for help in rescuing Joseph and Rosa. But what about you, Sukie? How can you bear working for Mr. Steele, the way he's treating your family?"

"I have to bear it." She looked hard at him, as if deciding how far to trust him. "Have you heard about a slave named Chloe Cooley?"

"I didn't just hear about her. I was there. I saw her struggle. She fought like a wildcat."

"Do you know why she fought like that?"

"No. I still don't understand why she was so desperate to stay here. What difference would it make to her? She'd still be a slave, whether in Upper Canada or New York State."

"Chloe was a house slave, like me. Her owner, Adam Vrooman, bought her from a man in Fort Erie and took her to his farm near Queenston. Vrooman had another slave, Tom. Chloe and Tom came to care for each other. Then Mr. Vrooman sold Tom. Chloe didn't know where he'd been taken. But she knew that if he ever got himself free, he'd come for her. That's why she wanted to stay in Queenston. If she was far away somewhere in the United States, Tom would never be able to find her. So I've made up my mind. No matter how bad he treats me, I'll give Mr. Steele no reason to sell me. I want to stay right here so that Joseph and Rosa can find me if they ever have a chance. I'll be the perfect slave. I won't burn my master's dinner or upset his chamber pot, though I can tell you what I'd like to do to him." With a grim smile, she picked up the big knife that she had been using to chop onions.

"You don't need to tell me. I'm going to see Simcoe right now."

The man with the cudgel shifted in his chair and glowered as Broken Trail left the kitchen.

# CHAPTER 9
# A Loophole in the Law

Lieutenant-Governor Simcoe's makeshift residence at Navy Hall was neither a tent nor a house, but something in between. Although the walls and roof were canvas, it had a wooden floor and its furniture was as fine as that in any English stately home.

The Governor and his lady were eating breakfast at a table spread with a white linen cloth. On it were china plates and platters heaped with food. Simcoe rose from his chair as soon as Broken Trail entered. His eyes took in Broken Trail's rifle and carrying basket.

"What happened?" he asked, before Broken Trail had said a word.

"I have left Mr. Steele's house."

"Yes, yes. I see."

Mrs. Simcoe set down her teacup. "John, please introduce this young man."

At this reminder, Simcoe presented Broken Trail as Captain Brant's deputy from the Six Nations. A soldier standing by pulled out a chair for him. When he was seated, Mrs. Simcoe offered him a cup of tea and a plate of scones.

Broken Trail took a sip and a nibble and then began to tell the Governor and Mrs. Simcoe what had happened. Mrs. Simcoe shuddered at his account of the chamber pot accident. They exchanged horrified glances while he described how Mr. Steele had ordered Joseph to beat his daughter with a buggy whip. When Broken Trail had finished, Mrs. Simcoe raised her handkerchief to wipe a tear from her cheek.

Simcoe turned pale. "My wife and I have six little girls."

"Six!"

"Yes, six daughters. We treasure each and every one. When I was appointed Lieutenant-Governor, my wife and I had to leave the four oldest back in England to be cared for by relatives and servants. Leaving them was very hard. Our oldest, Eliza, was only seven."

"We brought Sophia and our baby boy with us," Mrs. Simcoe added. "Sophia was two years old and Frank three months when we left England. Our new baby, Katherine, was born here in Niagara just six months ago. She's our little Canadian child."

Simcoe clenched his fist. "If anyone laid a hand on one

of my daughters, I'd personally take a buggy whip to him. Joseph is a brave man. We must help him."

"But how?" asked Broken Trail. "He's a slave for life. So is his daughter."

"I know. I've done my best to rid Upper Canada of slavery. It will happen, but not in our time." For a minute, the Governor sat with his fingers pressed to his forehead. "The new law has a loophole that might help. You say that Mr. Steele is selling Joseph and the girl to a jobber who will take them to the United States."

"That's his plan."

"Where are they now?"

"I don't know. Sukie, Joseph's wife, told me that men from Mr. Steele's warehouse took them away in the middle of the night."

"His men probably took them to the warehouse. It's a building down by the water where he stores goods that come here by ship. Mr. Steele deals in rum from the Caribbean, china and glassware from England and rice from South Carolina. His warehouse is the likeliest place for his men to keep Joseph and his daughter locked up until the jobber takes them away. Now, listen carefully. Three things are necessary for the loophole to work. First, Mr. Steele must sell them. Second, they must be taken out of Upper Canada. Third, they must come back."

"I don't understand. If they came back, they'd be no better off than before. They'd still be slaves."

"Here's where the loophole comes in. The new law says: 'Nor shall any Negro or other person who shall come or be brought into this Province after the passing of this Act, be subject to the condition of a Slave.'"

Mrs. Simcoe set down her teacup. "Surely it can't be that simple. If it is, then all a slave has to do to gain his freedom is escape across the border and then come back."

"You're right, my dear. It isn't so simple. That's because the new law makes an exception in the case of slaves who were already their owner's property *before* the new law came into force. Such slaves remain his property for the rest of their lives, no matter where he takes them. But that exception doesn't exist for a new owner who buys a slave *after* the new law came into effect. If Mr. Steele sells Joseph and Rosa today, the buyer won't have the benefit of that exception. If the buyer takes Joseph and Rosa out of this province and then they come back, they are slaves no longer. The moment they re-enter Upper Canada, their shackles fall off."

Broken Trail scratched his head. "So, I don't want to rescue them right now. I have to wait until the jobber takes them to the United States. Then I help them escape and come back here to Upper Canada."

"Exactly. But there's one other thing you must do for this loophole to work. That is, you must get hold of the bill of sale for Joseph and Rosa. That's essential, because it will have the date on it proving the jobber bought them *after* July 9. I frankly have no idea how you can manage that."

"I'll find a way. But first, I must find Joseph and Rosa."

"Good. You can start now. I'll send a soldier to Brant's Ford to deliver my letter to Captain Brant. Unfortunately, that's the limit to what I can do to help. You see, I represent King George. The king is not above the law. As his representative, I must be careful in my own observance. To tell you about the loophole is as much as I can do."

"So I'm on my own."

"Yes. But I'm confident that you have the skills and the courage to succeed."

Broken Trail did not disagree. After that, they talked about other things. Mrs. Simcoe described her first experience of eating moose lips while Broken Trail finished off the plate of scones.

# CHAPTER 10
## The Search Begins

The man with the cudgel was no longer there when Broken Trail returned to Mr. Steele's home. Sukie was alone, kneading a lump of dough at the kitchen table. White flour dusted her dark hands.

"Do you have any news?" she asked.

"I do. Important news." Wasting no time, he told her what Lieutenant-Governor Simcoe had told him and explained how the loophole worked. As he talked, she kept on kneading the dough, glancing up from time to time as he outlined the steps by which Joseph and Rosa would gain their freedom.

Once or twice she grunted, "Uh-huh." Although he did his

best to sound confident of success, she did not look convinced. When he had finished speaking, she lifted her hands from the dough. "How can you free Joseph and Rosa if you don't even know where they are? And what about the other things you need to do, like getting your hands on those bills of sale? My goodness! I don't see how one person can do all that. And even if your plan works so that Joseph and Rosa are freed, I'll remain a slave. We still won't be together as a family." She shook her head from side to side and muttered, "It will never work."

"As soon as they're free, they can start earning money to buy you. Then they can set you free. Mr. Steele's a businessman. He won't turn down a chance to make a profit."

"That's the truth! But I don't see how they can ever raise enough money."

Although everything she said was exactly what he feared, her doubts made him more determined. He seized her flour-covered hands. "Sukie, I will find Joseph and Rosa. I will bring them back to you, and I will bring them back free. I give you my word." He released her hands. She said nothing, but he saw a glimmer of hope in her eyes. "I'm going now to look for them. They're probably locked up in Mr. Steele's warehouse. If they are, I'll sneak inside to tell them what I'm doing."

"How will you get inside?"

"That's what I have to figure out."

• • •

Mr. Steele's warehouse stood close to the water at the bottom of the slope that led up to Navy Hall. On the slope was a sumac grove from which he could watch the warehouse without being seen. Broken Trail crept in among the bushes, took his carrying basket from his back, laid his rifle on the ground and sat down. The sumacs' green leaves shaded him from the blazing sun.

The warehouse was a sprawling, one-storey frame building that looked as though it had been cobbled together at different times as Mr. Steele's business grew. Additions had been tacked on to the main building arbitrarily, like they had been built with no plan. There were even newer additions tacked onto some of the original additions, each with a separate entrance. Were those sections connected inside, so that one entrance gave access to all? Or would he need to break into each one individually? He counted. The warehouse had nine sections. Which one held Joseph and Rosa, if they were there at all?

It was a warm July day. Raspberry Moon, the Oneidas called it. In the woods on the faraway shore of Oneida Lake, the girls would be picking raspberries with gathering baskets over their arms as they walked along shady paths. Little birds would be twittering in the undergrowth. Here, in the sumac grove, the birds were silent. Too hot to sing. Too hot even to move. Sweat ran down under Broken Trail's leather poncho. He took it off. Then the mosquitos began to bite.

Not much was happening at the warehouse. Outside the

door of one of the larger sections, four men were loading barrels onto a wagon. Three of the men were white and one was black. All were muscular, with great shoulders, chests, necks and arms. Broken Trail liked the way they worked together as a team.

Two yoked oxen waited patiently while the men dragged barrels from the warehouse on a sort of sled with wheels. It took two men to lift each barrel. Broken Trail counted twenty-four barrels to make up the full load. One of the white men climbed onto the seat of the wagon and cracked his whip. The oxen set off up the dirt road to Navy Hall. The other three men disappeared into the warehouse.

After a time, a workman carrying a bucket emerged from the warehouse. He walked down to the landing, dipped the bucket into the lake and carried it, dripping, into a shed that stood apart from the rest of the warehouse. A minute later, he came out with the empty bucket and went back into the main building.

The shed was large enough to hold two people. Maybe Joseph and Sukie were locked up there and the man had brought them water. Broken Trail wished he had a bucket of fresh, cool water. He would take a long drink and then splash the rest over his head and shoulders. He felt cooler just thinking about it.

If nothing happened during the day, he would wait in the sumac grove until after dark and then creep down to the shed. He wouldn't need to break in. If Joseph and Rosa were there, he could sneak up close and talk with them through the shed wall to let them know the plan.

He held onto this idea until the sun was halfway down the sky. Then the door to the warehouse's main building opened and Mr. Steele came out, followed by the man who had carried the bucket. The man entered the shed while Mr. Steele waited outside, looking back at the warehouse as if to be sure it wouldn't disappear in his absence.

A minute or two later, the man led from the shed a fine-looking horse, saddled up and ready to go. It was a handsome creature, dark reddish-brown with a black mane and tail—a better horse than Mr. Steele deserved! Broken Trail's envy changed to amusement as he watched the man assist Mr. Steele to mount, heaving him upward by his bottom as if he were a sack of flour. Horse and rider headed up the road. The man went back into the warehouse.

Broken Trail settled down again to wait. In the drowsy heat, it was hard to keep his eyes open. He was fighting sleep when a whistle shrieked, jolting him awake. He blinked his eyes, watching workmen emerge from the various parts of the building. The only black man among them was the worker who had been part of the team loading barrels onto the wagon. Broken Trail kept his eyes on that man. Was he free or a slave? In either case, any black man would surely be sympathetic to Joseph and Rosa's plight.

The black man was walking beside one of the white warehousemen. They appeared to be chatting, for their heads tipped toward each other from time to time. When they were halfway up the road to Navy Hall, Broken Trail put on his poncho, picked up his rifle and carrying basket and left the sumac grove. He followed the two men, keeping a good distance behind them. At the top of the hill, they parted with a friendly wave. As soon as the black man was walking alone, Broken Trail hastened to catch up to him.

"Pardon me," he called, stepping in front of him. "May I have a word with you?"

The man stopped and looked at Broken Trail, his eyes taking in the scalp lock, the deerskin clothes and the rifle. "What about?"

"It's about two people. A man called Joseph and his daughter, Rosa."

"What about 'em?" The man's eyes narrowed.

"Maybe you know where they are."

"You're asking me because I'm black, aren't you? You think I might get mixed up in some business that's not mine."

"No! You don't need to be involved." Broken Trail took a deep breath. "Please, just tell me if Joseph and the girl are in the warehouse."

The man looked him in the eye. "There's no such people in the warehouse. That's God's truth. There's no living creature in there except the rats." Then he turned and started to walk.

Broken Trail kept along beside him. "Are you sure? Are you absolutely sure? Joseph's wife, Sukie, is beside herself with worry."

The man stopped again. "Have you been talking with Sukie?"

"Yes. I've given her my word I'd help them."

"So you're not working for Mr. Steele?"

"Never! Why would you think that?"

"Why wouldn't I? I don't know whether you count as white or Indian, but you sure aren't black."

"It doesn't matter what I am. I think Joseph and Rosa were taken to the warehouse. Is that where they are? Answer me, yes or no, and I'll trouble you no more."

"I told you the truth. They aren't there. I'm taking a chance just telling you this much. I work for Mr. Steele. I'm a free man. I earned my freedom by helping the British during the war. Mr. Steele don't pay me as much as he pays a white man, but it's still the best-paying work a man like me will ever find. I have a wife and five little ones to feed. I can't risk losing my position." A crafty look came into his eyes. "I told you the truth, that Joseph and the girl aren't in the warehouse."

"Go on."

"That's not to say they weren't never there."

"You mean they were, but they've gone?"

The man nodded. "When I came to work this morning, just past dawn, I saw them loaded into a cart and carried away. They were bound and gagged, but I recognized them."

"Where were they taken?"

"I don't know. But I can tell you that Queenston is where jobbers ship slaves over the river to sell in the United States.

If a jobber bought Joseph and the girl, Queenston's the place to look for them."

"Thank you. I'll never breathe a word of this to anybody."

"Forget you ever spoke with me or anybody who looks like me!"

"Forget? Why, I never set eyes on you in my entire life."

# CHAPTER 11

# Dragged from the River

Images flashed through his mind as he ran. He saw Joseph and Rosa tied hand and foot and thrown into a boat, just as Chloe Cooley had been. But it wouldn't be only them. The jobber would have a cargo of slaves to carry over the river. How many? Perhaps, with the addition of Joseph and Rosa, he now had a full load. If he did, the boat might leave at any time.

Maybe it was mad to feel such urgency. Joseph and Rosa might not be at Queenston. The man from the warehouse had made a suggestion, not a guarantee. But it was the only lead Broken Trail had. He kept on running.

Broken Trail ran along the grassy margin at the edge of the road, avoiding the beaten track, for the road from Newark to Queenston was not meant for moccasined feet. Rutted by wagon wheels and pitted by the hooves of horses and oxen, the mud on the road was baked hard as rock by the merciless sun.

As he ran, he watched for the path to his sister's cabin. When he saw the sign, H. COBMAN, he gave it a nod of greeting, wishing he had time to stop and tell Hope what he was doing. She would cheer him on. Hope hated slavery. A runaway slave would find a hiding place in her cabin. Right now, he didn't need a place for slaves to hide. He needed to find the place where slaves were already hidden.

He reached Queenston landing just as the sun dipped below the trees. A small crowd of men and women was gathered at the very spot where Chloe Cooley had made her fight to stay in Upper Canada. Standing in a circle, all were looking at something that lay on the ground. The men had taken off their hats.

Broken Trail slipped between the shoulders of two onlookers to see what everyone was looking at. It was the nearly naked, broken body of a black man.

"Four in ten days!" A bystander shook his head. "All of them Negroes."

"All of them broken and bashed like this," another added.

Their voices were hushed, as if this were a funeral.

"Maybe they were trying to escape by jumping from a

boat taking them across the river," one woman suggested. "But they couldn't swim."

"No," said the man who had spoken first. "Simple drowning, even after a struggle, can't cause such terrible injuries. Skin and flesh torn away. Just about every bone in this man's body is broken. He must have gone over the falls onto the rocks below."

"In that case, all of them went over the falls," another bystander said gruffly. "Because all the bodies were as battered as this poor devil's."

A white-haired, older man spoke solemnly. "It was suicide. They took their own lives out of despair when they learned that the new law would never set them free."

"Look!" said the man with the gruff voice. "The new law wasn't proclaimed until July 9. The first three died before that date. They couldn't have known the new law wasn't going to free them. Maybe they had a reason to kill themselves, but that wasn't it."

After a delay in which people counted the days on their fingers, it was agreed that suicide failed to explain the first three deaths.

"Who were the four men?" Broken Trail asked, speaking for the first time. All eyes turned to him. "Did anybody recognize them?"

"When we dragged the bodies from the river, there wasn't enough left to recognize." The gruff-voiced man clapped his hat onto his head. "All that remains for us to do is bury this poor fellow. We can put his body in my shed, like we did the others, and take care of it in the morning."

As the body was carried off, everyone turned to walk away.

"Just a minute!" Broken Trail called. "Please! I'm looking for two black people who may have been brought here today. A man about forty and a girl of twelve. The man's tall with broad shoulders. The girl's tall for her age, but skinny. They belonged to a Newark man who sold them to a jobber. I think the jobber plans to take them across the river to sell at a slave auction. Has anybody seen them?"

Everyone stopped and looked at him. Several shook their heads and muttered, "Sorry."

One man gave a snort. "It sounds like Skinner's back in town."

The crowd dispersed, except for a middle-aged man with greying hair tied at the nape of his neck. He approached Broken Trail. "I've seen you before. Aren't you the young fellow who works for Joseph Brant?"

"I help Captain Brant with treaty negotiations and other things."

"During the war, I was one of Brant's volunteers. Only half his regiment were Mohawk warriors—the rest of us were Loyalists who'd been driven from our homes. Brant's a brave man. I was proud to serve under him." He paused, looking Broken Trail up and down the way everybody always did. "If you've just arrived and need a place to sleep, I can offer you supper and a bed."

Broken Trail hesitated. It was already getting dark. He couldn't search any further tonight. "Thank you. That's very kind."

"If you're a friend of Captain Brant, you're a friend of mine." He shook Broken Trail's hand. "I'm Peter Shaw."

"My name is Broken Trail, or Moses Cobman, depending on where I am and who I'm talking to."

"I'll call you Broken Trail."

• • •

Shaw's home was a cabin built of squared logs with a fenced vegetable patch in front and a woodpile at the side. A candle shone in the window.

Inside, Mrs. Shaw had a tea kettle steaming on the hob and a pot of stew simmering over the fire. She welcomed Broken Trail with a smile. "Peter brings home strangers all the time. Everyone is welcome here."

After they had eaten supper, she lit a second candle and withdrew to the cabin's other room carrying a book.

"She likes to read," Shaw explained. "That's a weakness she has."

Broken Trail welcomed the chance to talk. Shaw was also eager for conversation, especially about the battles and campaigns of the war in which Britain lost her Thirteen Colonies and the Loyalists lost their homes. He was disappointed to learn that Broken Trail had been too young to fight, but made up for his disappointment by treating his guest to a detailed account of the Battle of Oriskany, which seemed to be the highlight of his war.

Eventually, Broken Trail brought the conversation around to the subject of his quest. "What can you tell me about the jobber who buys up slaves to sell in the United States? I heard somebody say, 'It sounds like Skinner's back.'"

"Jonas Skinner. He buys them up. When he has a full load—about twenty—he hires a boat to ship them across the river. On a dark, moonless night, you can hear the oars splashing. A friend of mine who saw it told me the Negroes were stacked like cordwood."

"Where does Skinner keep the slaves before he takes them across the river?"

Peter Shaw rubbed his nose thoughtfully. "I've no idea. When he comes to town, which is three or four times a year, he stays at Berry's Tavern. Frank Berry's a trader who deals in every kind of evil money can buy."

"Could Berry's Tavern be where Skinner holds the slaves until he has a full load?"

"It isn't big enough."

"Maybe there's an old barn on the property."

Shaw shook his head. "No. Berry's Tavern is right in town. I reckon Skinner has a place off in the woods where his men can come and go unseen. It has to be a secret location. Most folks around here are opposed to slavery. Many of us would help the slaves escape if we knew where Skinner keeps them."

"You mentioned Skinner's men. So he doesn't work alone?"

"He has three men working for him—brutes, I'd call them. They do the rough work while Skinner looks after the money. He's a scrawny little man—reminds me of a weasel. He wears a short coat and breeches like any ordinary working man. You'd never notice him, except he always carries a brown leather satchel with a strap over his shoulder, and he never lets go of it. I haven't seen him around here for quite a while. It's about time he showed up again." Shaw pulled a pipe and a tobacco pouch from his pocket. He crossed the room to the fireplace and lit his pipe with an ember from the fire. "Down at the landing, you asked whether anyone had seen two black people that you're looking for. May I ask why you want to find them?"

"They're a father and daughter, Joseph and Rosa. Their owner sold them to a jobber who'll take them to the United States to sell at auction. From what you've told me, I think Skinner may be the jobber who bought them. I think his men have brought them to Queenston."

Shaw puffed steadily on his pipe. "So you want to help them escape."

"Not just escape. There's a way I can help them become free, legally free, under the Law of Upper Canada. It's complicated."

"If there's any way I can help, let me know. My friend Roger Counter will help, too. You saw him tonight. It's his shed where they put the body to bury in the morning."

"Thank you. I may need your help. But first, I must find Joseph and Rosa."

"Then my advice is to search in the forest above the falls as well as below. Maybe there's a connection between Skinner's business and those bodies we pulled from the river."

Broken Trail shuddered at the thought. "That's a good idea. I won't give up until I find Joseph and Rosa. They must be somewhere."

"They can't be too far away, not if Skinner's shipping them from Queenston." Shaw knocked the ashes from his pipe into the fireplace. "You must be ready for a good night's sleep. I know I am." He pointed to a cot against the wall. "I think you'll find it comfortable enough."

# CHAPTER 12

# Where Have They Gone?

∽

In the morning, Broken Trail was wakened by Mrs. Shaw building up the fire to cook a pot of cornmeal mush. While they were eating, Shaw advised Broken Trail.

"Your best plan is to follow the road to the falls. Along the way, watch for paths that lead into the bush."

Broken Trail nodded. "A good idea. An abandoned cabin in the woods would make a perfect hiding place."

"There are quite a few of those. Do you know this part of the country?"

"I've never been here before."

"The road's called the Niagara Portage. Queenston's as far

as a ship can navigate up the Niagara River, so ships carrying freight bound for settlements on the north shore of Lake Erie have to unload here. Then the cargo is carried by wagon around the falls. At Fort Erie, it's loaded onto another ship for the rest of the journey."

While he was speaking, Mrs. Shaw brought cups of tea to the table and then sat down with her husband and Broken Trail. "You'll find the road mighty busy today," she said. "I stepped outdoors for a moment and saw a ship being un-loaded down at the landing."

"Sometimes the portage is busy, and sometimes there's scarcely a soul on it," said Shaw.

When Broken Trail had finished his tea and thanked the Shaws for their hospitality, he hoisted his carrying basket onto his back, picked up his rifle and started on his way.

• • •

Leaving Queenston, he shared the road with a caravan of lumbering, creaking Conestoga wagons and carts of various sizes pulled by oxen. Teamsters cracked their whips to warn the labouring oxen to keep moving. Broken Trail felt a stab of sympathy for the big, dumb beasts under their heavy yokes. It was a hot day. His skin felt sticky with sweat under his leather poncho, and the dust stirred up by the plodding oxen and turning wheels made his eyes itch.

On his left were the steep, rocky walls of the Niagara Gorge, where nothing bigger than a cliff swallow could have found a hiding place. He saw no point in searching the gorge for Joseph and Rosa.

On his right, to the north, lay forest and farms. Taking Shaw's advice, he watched for paths leading into the bush. The first one he followed took him half a mile north to a grove of hickory trees, and that was as far as it went. He returned to the road, which now was empty, the caravan already far ahead of him on its way to Fort Erie.

The next time he left the road was to explore an old lane where tall grass grew in ruts made by wagon wheels. This lane led him to the charred remains of a burned-out log cabin. Again, he returned to the road.

Broken Trail spent that whole day searching. Despite all his skill as a hunter, he found no trace of Joseph and Rosa. At dusk, he shot a rabbit and made camp. He cut up the rabbit and toasted its meat on green sticks over the fire. This was good food, caught and cooked by him—better for a warrior than the finest dinner prepared and served by slaves.

As the flames of his campfire died down, he stared into the glowing embers and thought about the challenges that lay ahead. From Peter Shaw, he had learned that the jobber's name was Jonas Skinner, that Skinner stayed at a place called Berry's Tavern when he visited Queenston and that he had three men working for him. Broken Trail had also learned that Skinner carried a leather satchel that he kept with him at all times. Why was the satchel so precious to him? Broken Trail was certain that he knew the reason.

Travelling about as he did, Skinner had no desk or cabinet in which to file important papers. The satchel must be where he kept them. Among those papers would be bills of sale recording the names of the slaves he bought and the dates on which he bought them. Those bills of sale would show that Skinner had purchased Joseph and Rosa after July 9. They were the evidence he needed to take advantage of the loophole in the new law. Broken Trail had to get that satchel or everything else would be in vain.

He spent a restless night tossing and turning, impatient to continue his search. At dawn, he began again. After several false starts, he came to a path that led him to an isolated cabin back in the bush, where an old man with long white hair and bristling whiskers smoked a pipe on the front step. The cabin door stood wide open. At one glance, Broken Trail knew that this was not the place he was looking for.

The old man looked up warily as he approached. "What do you want?" His tone made it clear that Broken Trail was not welcome.

"Sir, I'm looking for a place where a man might hide something—or somebody—that he didn't want others to see."

"Is that right?" The old man spat on the ground. "The only thing hiding here is me. I don't want no other company but my own. So I'll thank you to leave my property."

Happy to let the hermit enjoy his solitude, Broken Trail returned to the Niagara Portage to continue his search. Late in the day, he came upon a path that led to a spring of fresh water. He stopped there to make camp for the night.

During the night, the wind shifted to the south. When Broken Trail woke at dawn, he heard in the distance the rumble of Niagara Falls. He stamped out any remaining embers of his campfire and returned to the road to resume his search.

At midday, the roar of raging water drew him to the brink of the gorge. The green water foamed as the river hurled itself into a maelstrom far below him. Round and round the torrent spun, a black hole at its core. Broken Trail knew about whirlpools, although he had never seen one before. He was wondering how deep the hole might be when, suddenly, a tree trunk shot straight up from its depths. He blinked. The tree had been a giant of the forest, a spruce or pine, yet the whirlpool tossed it up like a piece of cordwood and then sucked it down again. With a shudder, he stepped back from the brink.

# CHAPTER 13

# The Maid of the Mist

There was a rainbow in the mist when Broken Trail reached Niagara Falls. He stood on a flat rock a stone's throw from the top and did not move for some time. As he watched the torrent surge over the brink, he wondered what it would be like to ride a canoe over the falls. He pictured the bow of his canoe poised for an instant in the empty air, then tipping and plunging down into the rocks below.

Had anyone ever survived such a ride? He knew the legend of Lelawala, the Maid of the Mist. She had been a young widow. Inconsolable at the death of her husband and wanting to end her life, she paddled her canoe into the middle of the Niagara River. While she was singing her death song, the current caught hold and swept her canoe to the brink. At the very moment her canoe pitched over, she noticed that the sky was blue, the sun warm and the world beautiful. Suddenly, Lelawala wanted to live. But it was too late to change her mind. She tumbled from her canoe as it plunged. As she fell, she screamed.

In the cave that was his home behind the falls, Heno, the God of Thunder, heard Lelawala's scream. He reached, caught her in his arms and gently laid her upon the floor of the cave. He and his family cared for her in their home. In time she overcame her grief and fell in love with Heno's younger son. She became his wife. A son was born.

Later, according to the legend, evil forces destroyed the cave. Lelawala's family found a new home in the sky. But the echo of Heno's voice could still be heard in the thunder of Niagara Falls.

The thunder of the falls was real. Had there once been a cave behind them, a cave large enough to house Heno and his family? Maybe the legend of Lelawala was not just a story. Broken Trail knew that such legends often held answers to the most puzzling questions. He stood staring at the terrible beauty of the falls until the shimmering light of the setting sun turned the mist to gold. Perhaps it was a trick of the light, but through the moving wall of water he glimpsed a shadow that might be the mouth of a cave.

It was time to make camp for the night. Maybe tomorrow

he would find the trail that would lead him to Joseph and Rosa. Broken Trail sensed that he was getting close.

He chose a spot in the forest, close enough to the river to hear the rumble of the falls. Not wishing to attract notice, he did not light a fire. There were raspberry bushes close by, the plump berries ripe for picking. He popped raspberries into his mouth as he picked them and he ate the rest of the rabbit he had shot the day before. Then he made himself a bed of spruce boughs. As he lay listening to the echo of Heno's voice, the idea of a cave would not leave his mind. He had seen that shadow. If not a cave, then what lay behind that impenetrable wall of water?

CHAPTER 14

# The Limestone Slab

∽

The next day he found the trail he had been looking for. There was a spot where twigs had been moved, tiny pebbles rolled aside and bits of moss loosened. From these signs Broken Trail knew he would soon see footprints, and so he did—clumsy footprints such as no Oneida warrior would leave. The people who made these tracks had no idea how to elude followers.

He studied the footprints. There were two men wearing boots, one man wearing shoes and one barefoot person whose footprint was narrower than usual for a man. Unless he was wrong—and Broken Trail was seldom wrong when reading footprints—he had found the trail of four people:

Joseph, Rosa and two guards. This was no surprise; he had expected that sooner or later he would find their trail. What he had not expected was the direction in which they were going, for the footprints led not into the forest but toward the Niagara Gorge.

Step by step, he followed. A smear of mud and a dislodged stone told him where someone had fallen. Then, stuck on a brier thorn, he found a scrap of white lace—just like the lace exposed at the cuff of Joseph's red velvet livery.

The trail brought him to the edge of the gorge, close to the brink of the falls. Below him was a steep and narrow path. Broken Trail was not afraid of heights. Even so, as he navigated the path, he avoided looking down at the chaos of broken limestone slabs below. The rocks under his feet were slippery with spray.

He was soaking wet from the spray by the time he reached the bottom, where water raged around huge chunks of limestone at the base of the falls. Some chunks were the size of his sister's log cabin.

He looked up. It was then that he noticed the great limestone ledge over which the torrent poured. It projected like a shelf from the top of the rock face, giving what was below it a scooped-out appearance. The ledge looked like the same kind of rock as the huge chunks at the bottom of the falls. *Long ago*, he thought, *those rocks at the bottom must have broken off from the ledge above.*

The torrent of falling water, so thick and impenetrable in

the middle of the falls, was thin and ragged at the edge. When he peered, half through the water and half around it, he saw a wide, tall shadow on the rock face. It was as wide and tall as Mr. Steele's two-storey house. If this shadow was a cave mouth, then the cave must be huge. But it might not be a cave. Just as likely, it was merely a depression in the rock wall behind the falls. The mist and spray made Broken Trail unsure of what he was looking at.

Two things he knew for sure. First, Joseph, Rosa and two guards had descended this path. Second, the trail ended here. On Broken Trail's left was the seething maelstrom at the base of the falls. On his right was the rocky cliff he had just descended. Directly in front of him was a great slab of creamy grey limestone. It was about one foot thick, five feet wide and seven feet high. It stood on end, looking as though it had been erected there as a barrier. Yet it was not much of a barrier, because there was room at one edge for a man to walk around to reach the other side.

Maybe it had simply fallen from the cliff above and happened to land upright on one end. Whether it had been placed there by nature or by man, half a dozen strong fellows pushing at the same time could topple it over, the way troublesome youths sometimes toppled gravestones in a cemetery.

He sensed danger. What was on the far side of the slab? Not much, he decided, for ten paces beyond the slab rose the rocky face of the Niagara Escarpment. Broken Trail pressed the palm of his hand against the stone. It felt rough and warm. He listened attentively. At first, all he could hear was the roar of the falls. Then, from the other side of the slab came a sound that was different and distinct. A snore. A loud and powerful snore. It was followed by another.

What a strange place to take an afternoon nap! Broken Trail hesitated. What should he do? Snorers sometimes woke themselves up. For a moment the snoring stopped, then started again as loudly as before. Broken Trail waited for something more to happen.

A long time seemed to go by. His training as a warrior had prepared him for vigils such as this. Once, on a warpath, he had waited silent and motionless all night for the signal to attack a village at dawn. Broken Trail held his rifle ready. But why wait for the other person to make a move? This was the best chance he was likely to have.

Carefully placing each foot, he edged around the slab, as stealthily as a wolf closing in on its prey. Then he saw the man. The snorer was lying on his back, his arms and legs sprawled on the flat rock. He was a long-limbed, loose-jointed giant of a man who looked as though the parts of his body had not been properly fitted together. His mouth gaped open. His eyes, under his heavy brows, were closed, and his rifle lay beside him on the ground. The scuffed toes of his big, black boots were pointing up. All around him lay a litter of chicken bones, not a shred of meat left on them.

Broken Trail suppressed a laugh. There were enough bones

lying about to make a skeleton for a whole chicken. The man had feasted well. But Broken Trail's amusement lasted for only a moment before he asked himself who had brought a cooked chicken to this place. This was a serious question. The man could not have cooked the chicken himself, for there was no sign of a fire. Peter Shaw had told Broken Trail that the jobber had three men working for him. If the sleeper was one, where were the other two?

The next thing Broken Trail noticed was a deep fissure in the rock face of the escarpment. It was only a few steps beyond the sleeper, and it was an opening wide enough to let a man walk through. There were many footprints of people going in, few of people coming out.

Suddenly Broken Trail had no doubt about what he had found. To reach the opening, all he had to do was sneak past the guard. Or shoot him.

He raised his rifle. It would be simple to shoot the man, but that would be a cowardly act unworthy of a warrior. Not only that, but what would happen if the guard's companions came back and found him dead? They would realize what had occurred and suspect that the killer had entered that hole and was still inside.

Of course, he could dispose of the body by throwing it into the river. But if the others returned to find the guard missing, it would rouse their suspicion as much as if they found him dead.

Sooner or later, the others were certain to arrive. If Broken

Trail acted right now, while the man lay sleeping, nobody would have the least idea that there was an intruder in the hiding place. He raised his hand to his chest to feel the shape of the amulet he wore under his leather shirt. It was a small doeskin bag packed with the hair and one fang of a wolverine, his *oki*, the spirit guardian that would keep him safe. While he felt the amulet's comforting shape, he breathed a prayer to the Invisible Spirits who had guided him here.

As he tiptoed past the man, whose loud snores continued without interruption, he was careful where he trod, lest the sleeper be wakened by the sound of feet crunching brittle chicken bones. Cautiously Broken Trail slipped through the opening in the rock.

Stepping into darkness from the bright sunlight outside, he could see nothing. He could hear nothing but the thunder of the falls, feel nothing but rough rocks under his moccasined feet and the wind that pushed against him from somewhere ahead in the dark. He stood still, waiting until his eyes adjusted, and then slowly he advanced into the narrow passage. With every step, the roar of the falls increased until his head pounded and his ears rang.

Then he saw light ahead.

# CHAPTER 15

# The Plan

Broken Trail stumbled out of the dark passage into a cavern filled with light. The light was steady, neither wavering like candlelight nor flickering like the light of a fire. It had an eerie underwater quality, with a tinge of green. He stood blinking for a moment. When his eyes had adjusted to the shock of so much light, he saw a group of men, women and children sitting on the cavern floor.

He looked for Rosa and Joseph, and there they were. He let out his breath in a whistle of relief. Rosa, in her outgrown white gown, was hunched over with her arms wrapped around her bony knees. Next to her sat Joseph. There was a rip in the sleeve of his red velvet coat, and the ruffles of his shirt were no longer snowy white.

With them were ten other captives: four men, three women and three children. One of the women had skin that was lighter than the others', and the little boy sitting beside her was fairer still. All the others were black. The second child was a girl about eight years old, and the third was a boy of ten or eleven. He sat apart from the rest of the group.

At first no one noticed Broken Trail's presence, for they all sat facing the wall of down-rushing water, staring at it from the inner side. Although the barrier of water did not block the light, it blocked everything else, so that the people sitting on the cavern floor were looking at it but saw nothing beyond. The way they sat, motionless, reminded him of a concourse of gulls on an ice floe or a herd of buffalo in a blizzard, all staring straight ahead in the same direction. They sat as still as if they had been carved from wood.

It was the boy, sitting apart from the group, who first happened to turn his head and notice Broken Trail. The boy sprang to his feet and pointed at him. Broken Trail could not hear his shout, for the wind whipped his words away. Yet, others must have heard, for most of them swivelled to take a look.

Joseph and Rosa jumped up. "Praise the Lord!" Joseph's deep voice was audible not over the noise of the wind and the water, but somehow within that noise and yet distinct from it. In an instant all were standing, except for a young woman in a yellow calico gown. She sat with one leg straight out in front of her, her ankle and lower leg wrapped in a makeshift bandage.

The people in the cave crowded around Broken Trail. Joseph called out, "Moses, I had faith you would find us!" He shouted other words, like "deliverance," "heaven-sent" and "Moses has come again."

The captives did not look impressed. They stared at Broken Trail with more curiosity than admiration. He didn't blame them for their lack of enthusiasm. He knew what he looked like, standing there in his soggy deerskin clothes with his hair in a limp scalp lock. He was no Moses, not like the one in the Bible. But Joseph was right about one thing: Broken Trail had come there to lead them out of slavery.

The captives turned to one another. They gestured with their hands and shrugged their shoulders. Their lips moved. Then, after a few minutes, most of them abandoned the effort to hear or be heard above the roaring wind and thundering water. One by one, they lost interest in Broken Trail and sat back down on the cave floor.

Rosa and Joseph did not sit down. As soon as they had Broken Trail to themselves, they began speaking at the same time. In Broken Trail's left ear, Joseph asked, "Have you seen Sukie?" In his right, Rosa yelled, "How is Mama?"

"I saw her three days ago, just before starting to search for you. She's fine," he shouted to them both. "She's doing the housework as well as the cooking for Mr. Steele. The extra work doesn't trouble her. She's more worried about you, and not knowing if you'll ever be together again."

"That's what troubles Rosa and me the most." Joseph's brow furrowed. "I'm afraid the three of us will be parted forever, unless there's a miracle."

"It won't need a miracle, because I have a plan." Broken Trail looked around, wondering if there were somewhere the noise wouldn't drown out his words.

Joseph seemed to understand. "It's quieter at the back." He gestured toward the rear of the cavern, where the rock wall was riven with cracks. Against the back wall, three wooden barrels stood in a row.

Broken Trail, Joseph and Rosa walked to the back of the cave and formed a huddle. It wasn't much quieter there. Broken Trail cupped his hands around his mouth and spoke as loudly as he could without actually shouting. "Sukie will wait for you. She won't run away or give Mr. Steele any reason to sell her. She'll be the perfect servant so that you'll find her waiting there when you return."

"I pray for that without ceasing." Joseph's eyes brightened. "You said you have a plan. What is it?"

"It depends on a loophole in the new law. Governor Simcoe explained it to me. The new law makes it illegal to bring a slave into Upper Canada. If anyone tries, that slave becomes a free person as soon as he or she crosses the border."

"I already knew that, and it's good as far as it goes. But it doesn't help us folks who are already enslaved."

"That's the problem. Nothing could change for you and Rosa as long as Mr. Steele was your lawful owner. But now he's sold you. That changes everything. I think your new owner is a jobber named Jonas Skinner. His men took you from Mr. Steele's warehouse."

Joseph nodded. "Two men. They tied us up and brought us here. A third man was on guard outside the cave. Rosa and I heard them talk about the man they work for. They called him Skinner."

"Skinner buys up slaves for auction in the United States. He probably owns every person here." Broken Trail waved his arm in the direction of the group sitting on the cave floor. "He bought you and Rosa, and likely the others, after the new law came into effect. That's important, because Skinner doesn't have the full rights that Mr. Steele had. If he takes you out of Upper Canada and then you come back, under the new law you cross the border into freedom."

"Is that what you call a loophole?"

"Yes. It's a hole you can slip through because Skinner did not own you before the new law came into effect."

Joseph shook his head. "I wish I knew how to read. Then maybe I'd understand how white people can play such tricks with words."

*Exactly!* Broken Trail thought to himself. That was the reason Thayendanegea had sent him to school—so he would understand the tricks with words that went into every treaty that took away more and more of his adoptive people's land.

"What if our new owner has us arrested after we've come back, and he tells the judge that we're his property?" Joseph asked.

"If Skinner understands the new law, he won't waste his time. But suppose he did have you arrested. Then you'd show the judge the bill of sale with the date right on it that proves he did not own you before the new law was passed."

"Bill of sale!" Joseph's eyes widened. "How do I get my hands on that?"

"Here's the next part of my plan. Skinner carries a satchel with a strap over his shoulder, and he never lets go of that satchel. It must be where he keeps his business papers, including bills of sale."

"If he never lets go of his satchel, how can we get those bills of sale?"

"I'll steal them. When I was a boy, I learned how to sneak up on a grouse's nest so stealthily that I could steal her eggs from under her, and she'd never know."

"Really?" Rosa's eyes narrowed, as if she didn't believe his story.

"Really."

"You found us," Joseph said slowly. "That took great skill."

"To follow your trail took skill. But when I came to the cave's entrance and found the guard fast asleep, it was more than my skill that helped me."

"Fast asleep! A miracle."

"Maybe. But there's another explanation. It's a warm day,

and he'd just had a good meal. There were chicken bones scattered all around. Somebody brought him a roast chicken. There's no sign of a cooking fire. I reckon they didn't want to take a chance that someone would see the smoke."

"Roast chicken!" Rosa's eyes went large and round. "I wish they'd bring us a roast chicken."

Broken Trail had not thought about this. "How do you get your food?"

Joseph pointed to the three barrels that stood in a row against the rock wall. "Apples in one barrel. Potatoes in the second. Salt pork in the third. After a time, you get used to eating raw potatoes. It's too wet to have a cooking fire."

"At least they don't starve you. A small kindness."

"Kindness has nothing to do with it. We have to appear healthy to fetch a good price at the slave auction. If it looks like we won't make the owner any money . . ." Joseph looked toward the woman with the bandaged leg. "I'm worried about what they might do to Mandy. She cut her foot on a rock when the men were dragging her down that steep path from the top. She was barefoot. Mandy told me the cut seemed like nothing at the time. But now her foot and lower leg are swollen and she can't walk."

Broken Trail eyed the bandage. It was dirty and poorly wrapped. "I'll look at it. Maybe I can help."

"You? I didn't know you were a medical man."

"Every Oneida warrior knows how to look after wounds, and I've learned new treatments from time to time. If you have salt pork, apples and potatoes in those barrels, there are three kinds of poultices I can make.

"But before I look at the woman's foot, I want to examine these cracks." He laid his hand upon a break in the rock wall. "We must find a way out."

"I've looked at every crack." Joseph pointed to one fissure that was wide enough for a man his size to enter. "I tried that one. After crawling fifty feet, I found a dead body partly covered by a cave-in. The fallen rocks blocked the tunnel. All I could do was say a prayer and leave the body there." He sighed. "Maybe I could have moved some of the rocks, but the body had been there for a long time."

"One grave is as good as another as long as the spirit has gone to a better place. Whether we call it Heaven or the Land Without Trouble doesn't matter."

"Amen. That's the truth," said Joseph. "I believe that, on your way here, you had a guardian angel watching over you."

*A guardian angel?* Broken Trail's *oki* had yellow teeth, a rank smell and the physical form of a wolverine. It was nothing like the angels in Bible stories. But that didn't matter.

"You're right." He smiled. "I do have a guardian angel. It brought me safely here, and it's not going to abandon me now."

CHAPTER 16

# Savage Medicine

✑

After Broken Trail had examined the cracks and crannies of the back wall, Joseph and Rosa took him to the front of the cave. He looked down into the gap between the edge of the cave floor and the wall of moving water. Twenty feet below him, the water foamed and swirled over huge, jagged rocks. Seeing them so close, with the spray flying in his face, he realized at once that a tumble from where he stood would be just as deadly as from the top of the falls. The dead men dragged from the river at Queenston could have fallen, jumped, or been pushed from this very spot.

Joseph laid a hand on his arm. "Stay away from the edge. That's not how you want to leave this cave."

"I agree." Broken Trail shuddered. "The only way we can escape is through a crack in the rock. I want another look at the back wall."

"You may not have much time before the other guards return. When there's just one at the entrance, it means the other two have gone to collect more slaves."

"How long does that usually take?"

"It depends on how far the men have to go to pick them up."

"I'll keep watch at the entrance while you explore," said Rosa. "If they come back, I'll run fast to warn you. There are plenty of cracks where you can hide."

"I can see that. Dozens big enough to hide in. But is there even one that leads to a way out of here?"

Joseph pointed to the back of the tunnel. "The best one I discovered led to the tunnel where I found the dead man. We can't use it because the rockfall that killed him has it completely blocked."

"If we can't find a way out, then we'll make one. Joseph, you had just your bare hands as tools. I have this." He pulled his tomahawk from his belt. One end of its steel head was a hatchet blade, and the other was shaped like a curved pick-axe. "Watch this!" He aimed the pick end at a narrow crack and struck hard. The tomahawk's head disappeared into the crack. When he pulled it out, a mass of shattered stone flew out with it. A chip struck Rosa's cheek.

"Ouch!" She pressed her hand to the cut. A trickle of blood ran down her fingers.

"I'm sorry!" said Broken Trail.

"Let me see!" Joseph gently pulled Rosa's hand from the cut. "It's not deep. If you press your fingers to it, you'll stop the bleeding."

Broken Trail picked up a chunk of the rock. "See? This isn't limestone. Look at the way it comes apart in layers. It crumbles."

"I noticed that. The roof of the cave is limestone, but underneath is this darker, softer rock." Joseph gave Broken Trail's tomahawk a keen look. "With a tool like that, you could widen a crack to make a tunnel to the outside."

"Show me where to start and I'll set to work. There's plenty of daylight left."

"Wait until morning. The light is starting to fade."

"Why wait? It'll be dark inside a tunnel whether it's day or night."

"You need to search in daylight so you can see light ahead. If there is light."

"That makes sense. I'll wait till morning." Broken Trail glanced toward the people sitting on the cave floor, staring at the wall of plunging water. There was the woman in the yellow calico gown, propped on her elbows with her bandaged leg stretched out in front of her. "While there's still enough light, I'll see if I can help the woman with the bad leg."

"You mean Mandy. I'll take you to her."

When Broken Trail approached, Mandy's eyes were half closed. He knelt at her side. "Mandy, Joseph told me about your injury. I think I can help you."

She opened her eyes fully. "From the look of you, I'd say you've been living with the Indians. I've heard that savage medicine has cures the rest of the world knows nothing about."

"Let me see your leg. Then I'll tell you what 'savage medicine' can do."

Broken Trail carefully untied the bandage, which reached from her instep to her knee. The bandage looked as though it was made of strips torn from a homespun shirt. The wound oozed pus. Mandy turned her face away. From the smell, Broken Trail knew that gangrene would soon set in. But it wasn't too late to save her leg—and her life.

Broken Trail glanced at the food barrels. "I'll make a poultice from some of that salt pork they feed you. Salt draws infection out of a wound."

Rosa started toward the barrels. "How much do you need?"

"A piece big enough to cover the wound and the skin around it. And it needs a fresh bandage."

While Rosa ran to get the salt pork, Joseph took off his velvet jacket and then his white shirt with its now limp and shabby ruffles. He ripped the shirt into bandage strips. In a few minutes, Rosa returned with the piece of salt pork. Broken Trail pressed it to Mandy's leg.

"How does that feel?"

Mandy gasped. "It stings!"

"Good, that means the flesh is still alive." He wrapped her leg with strips of Joseph's shirt to hold the salt pork in place.

"I'll look at it again tomorrow. When your wound starts to heal, there's a poultice I can make with rotten apples to soothe the skin."

"Most of the apples in the barrel are half rotten," said Joseph.

"That's just what we want." Broken Trail smiled at Mandy. "You eat the good half, and I'll mash the rotten half for a poultice."

Mandy smiled back. "I feel better already, just by thinking about it."

After leaving her, Broken Trail shared a supper of salt pork, raw potatoes and apples with Rosa and Joseph. As they ate, the greenish light that filtered through the wall of water faded to a shimmering grey. *The light comes from the moon*, he thought, remembering how full the moon had been only a few nights ago.

One by one, the captives lay down on the cave floor to sleep. Broken Trail remained awake for a long time, staring at the wall of water. What a day this had been! He had not only found Joseph and Rosa, but ten more slaves held captive in this cave. It was up to him to rescue them all. If there was no tunnel, he would make one. *In the morning*, he thought to himself, *I'll see what needs to be done.*

# CHAPTER 17

# The Guards Return

"Hide!" Rosa shouted, shaking Broken Trail awake. "The guards are back!"

Broken Trail raced to a cranny in the back wall. He was in his hiding place before he could see who had entered the cave, or before anyone entering could see him. With his body crammed into a crack in the rock, he could hear nothing but the roar of the wind and the thunder of the falls. If he turned his head, he could see the shimmering light that streamed through the moving wall of water.

His thoughts were furious. What was he doing here? It went against all his instincts and training to hide like a timid rabbit. He was a warrior. He had his rifle. If he were to step out from this crack in the rock, take aim and fire, he knew that he could shoot one of the guards. There were five able-bodied men in the cave who could rush the other two guards. Then all the captives could escape through the same hole from which they had been brought here, with no need to find a different way out.

And then?

That was the problem. The use of violence would turn the captives into fugitives. The law would pursue them. Slave catchers would round them up. Ordinary citizens would turn them in for the reward money. So forget about violence. Broken Trail knew he must be patient and stick with his plan. Only the loophole in the new law could give the captives real freedom, so that no one could ever rob them of their liberty.

Broken Trail shifted his position. He watched the light change from bright to dim to bright again. The dimness must have been caused by a passing cloud. It happened again. Bright to dim. Dim to bright. How much longer would he have to stay in hiding? The guards already had plenty of time to bring in the new captives and depart. Or was there some other reason for them to be in the cave? Maybe they knew there was an intruder. Maybe he had left a clue, dropped some little thing that the sentry found when he awoke. If so, the guards might be searching for him right now. He raised his rifle.

At that very moment, Rosa's face appeared. She saw the rifle pointed at her chest and gasped. "No! No!"

He immediately lowered the barrel, stammering. "I'm so sorry, I thought—"

She raised one hand. "It's all right. They've gone."

"They were in the cave so long."

"It took the guards a long time to untie the rope," she explained. "They brought in four more slaves. There was one long rope joining all of them together in a line, with the rope knotted around each person's neck. The guards took the rope away with them."

When Broken Trail emerged from his hiding place, he saw three men and one woman stretching their arms and rubbing their necks. There were gestures, frowns, nods and shouts as the new arrivals exchanged information with the captives who had been in the cave for a longer time. The newcomers looked around at the rock walls, the underside of the ledge that formed the cave roof and the plunging water that shut them off from the world beyond. After a while, they sat down on the cave floor with the others, facing the wall of water.

Mandy was not there. Broken Trail looked, and looked again. Mandy could not walk. Where had she gone? He turned to Joseph, but before he could ask, Joseph sighed. "Are you looking for Mandy? You won't find her. They threw her out of the cave."

It took a moment for Joseph's meaning to sink in. "You mean they killed her?"

"She's not the first. With her bad leg, she wouldn't make the jobber any profit at the slave auction."

Broken Trail shuddered at the thought of the jagged rocks tearing her body. Holding his features rigid, as a warrior should, he leaned toward Joseph and spoke loudly in order to be heard. "In Queenston, where I started looking for you and Rosa, I was told that the bodies of four black men had been dragged from the river."

"Just four?" Joseph shook his head. "There'll be more to fish out before they've got them all."

"I also heard there that the jobber makes a shipment across the river to New York State when he has about twenty slaves gathered to make up a load."

"Then it'll be a short load this time. There'll be just fifteen of us, unless he picks up a few more in the next couple of days."

"How do you know it'll be that soon?"

"The guards checked the food barrels this morning while you were hiding. I heard one say, 'There's just enough to feed this lot until we take them away. Skinner's already hired a boat.'"

"How long do you think the food will last?" Broken Trail asked.

"Maybe two days."

"Two days! We have no time to lose. I'll start now. Show me the best place to explore."

"Apart from the cave-in, I found one crack that may lead to something. Follow me."

Rosa went with them to the back wall of the cave. Joseph led them to a large crevice, high enough and wide enough for Broken Trail to pass through easily.

Broken Trail took a step in. "It looks good."

"The first twenty or thirty feet are no problem," said Joseph. "Then the walls close in. I went as far as I could, squeezing sideways, but I knew I'd be stuck if I went further. I didn't want to quit. Even though I couldn't see any light ahead, the air was fresh."

Rosa's eyes widened. "The fresh air must be coming from somewhere."

"You're right, Rosa." Joseph smiled. "It means the tunnel doesn't come to a dead end. So it's worth a look." He turned to Broken Trail. "You're thinner than me."

"I'll give it a try."

"May I come with you?" Rosa asked. "I'm thinner than both of you."

This was true. But Rosa was inexperienced and clumsy. If she came along, he'd end up carrying her back with a sprained ankle, or worse. "You're brave to offer, but you should stay here."

"You think I wouldn't be any help, but two pairs of eyes are better than one pair. You and I might notice something Daddy missed."

"Four eyes can't see any better than two eyes in the dark," Broken Trail protested.

"That's true," Joseph agreed. "But two explorers in a cave *is* safer than one. If you were hurt, Rosa could go for help."

Broken Trail hesitated. After a few moments, he gave in. "Very well." He turned to Rosa. "So long as you aren't afraid of the dark."

Rosa stuck out her chin. "I'm not afraid of anything."

# CHAPTER 18

# The Dark Tunnel

Broken Trail took with him his pouch, his knife and his tomahawk. Into the pouch he put two apples. The crevice that he and Rosa entered was tall enough for them to stand erect. Broken Trail led, Rosa followed. At first, there was enough light from behind for them to see a few paces ahead. After that, they progressed by touch in the darkness.

For a short distance, their shoulders easily cleared the side walls. Then, as Joseph had warned, the tunnel narrowed. Only by angling their bodies sideways could they squeeze between the walls.

"We're already farther than Daddy could have come," Rosa called out when they were about a hundred feet into the passage.

"You're right, Rosa. But it's as far as you and I can go unless I widen the passage." He reached forward, feeling for a crack or the edge of a chunk of rock he might pry free. What he found was a shoulder of stone protruding halfway across the tunnel. He pulled his tomahawk from his belt. His first blow with the pick produced no result. He struck again, twisting the handle as he pulled back. This time, a chunk of rock the size of his head broke loose. Broken Tail jumped back to avoid it landing on his feet.

Their progress was slow. Again and again, Broken Trail had to stop to enlarge the passage. His assault on the rock became a practised manoeuvre: strike, twist, pull.

The tunnel began to tilt upward, at first gradually but then sharply, so that they were climbing as they inched their way along. At the same time, the tunnel roof lowered, forcing them first to stoop and then to crawl on their hands and knees. The roof grew lower and lower until they were wriggling on their stomachs.

That was when the first drops of water came trickling through. *Drip. Drip.* The droplets ran down his scalp and the back of his neck, reminding him that this tunnel was right under the Niagara River. How many hundreds of tons of water were flowing above their heads, separated from them by a ceiling of crumbing limestone, while he and Rosa wriggled onward like worms in total darkness?

Behind him, he heard the sound of Rosa's breathing. It was not steady breathing, but harsh panting interrupted by

*Umph!* and *Ow!* from time to time. He heard it clearly, just as he heard the water dripping—distinct sounds that stood out from the background roar.

"How is it with you, Rosa?"

"Fine! Except I'm hungry."

"Hungry? So am I!" It must have been hours since they last ate. "We'll stop to eat an apple as soon as there's somewhere we can sit up."

He wasn't sure there would be such a place. But after they squirmed on their bellies a few yards further, the roof began to rise and they were able to crawl again on their hands and knees. Soon, the space widened so that they came to a place where they could stop to eat. Broken Trail sat with his back against the tunnel wall.

"Did you notice that the dripping has stopped?" asked Rosa.

"So it has! That means we're no longer under the river." Broken Trail took the apples from his pouch and held one out toward where he thought Rosa was sitting. "Here's your apple."

"Where is it?"

"I'm holding it out to you."

He felt a tap on his wrist, and then the apple was taken from his hand. He heard the crunch as she took a bite.

"Did you know that there are caves down south with rivers underground where the fish have no eyes?" Rosa asked. "When Daddy was butler in a big house in Virginia, he knew another slave who came from Alabama. Daddy's friend had seen those fish. They had no eyes, just a mark like a scar where eyes should be."

"Living in the dark all their lives, those fish didn't need eyes. Eyes would be of no use to them."

She laughed. "Just like my sharp eyes are no use to us in this tunnel. But my nose works fine." She sniffed. "I can't see anything, but I smell earth." She sniffed again. "I smell grass."

Broken Trail inhaled. "So can I! We've been climbing for a long time. It can't be much farther before this tunnel breaks through someplace above the falls. Let's go!"

They set off on their hands and knees. After a few yards, the ceiling lowered abruptly. With a sharp crack, Broken Trail's skull met a rock and he felt the shock of bone on stone. He saw stars and heard a ringing in his ears.

"How are you?" Rosa sounded worried. "Is something wrong?"

He tried to laugh. "I just gave my head a bump." He paused, thinking over what he should do next. His voice was sober when he continued. "Rosa, I need to clear more space over-head, but I can't do it unless I lie on my back and reach up to knock down some of the rock. Doing this may cause a cave-in. Listen carefully. Before I start, I want you to crawl backwards to move yourself safely out of the way. If this goes wrong, you must return to the cave to get help."

"All right! But it's not going to go wrong."

For a moment, the rumble of the falls was all he heard.

Then came her shout from farther back in the tunnel. "I'm out of the way. Go ahead and smash some rock!"

Lying on his back, Broken Trail had just enough room to wield the tomahawk. He reached it up and over his head, stretching his arms in the direction he wanted to go. Working in this position, it was impossible to strike with much force. But could he still use too much? If he pulled down a really big rock, there was a good chance it would crush him.

"*Oki*, help me," he prayed. Then he raised his tomahawk with a two-handed grip and struck one sharp blow, driving the pick into the rock. With a twist of the handle, he pulled down a chunk of stone and a clatter of fragments that landed mere inches beyond his head. Rock dust stung his eyes.

"How are you?" Rosa called.

"Good!"

For a moment he lay still, blinking the dust from his eyes. Then he squirmed a few feet farther and repeated the action. He did this a third time, and then a fourth, each time shoving the rough pieces of fallen rock to the sides and pushing the stone chips into whatever cracks and holes he could find.

Broken Trail's head throbbed from its collision with the rock. His arms and shoulders ached. But the darkness seemed less dark and the fresh breeze blew more strongly as he advanced.

Suddenly, the tunnel opened upon a small, clear space. Lying on his back, he saw sheer stone walls and, way above his head, a patch of light.

# CHAPTER 19

# The Errand

It felt like a great victory to have reached this place where they could see daylight overhead and also see each other. They stood up, stretched, stamped their feet and laughed out loud. It felt so good to not be crawling on their hands and knees.

Drops of sweat ran like tears through the dust on their cheeks. "Your hair's gone grey," said Broken Trail. It was true. The little cornrows of her black hair were coated with rock dust. It powdered the dark skin of her arms and face.

"You got a big bump on your head."

Broken Trail touched it gingerly. The soft, sore lump was

just to one side of his scalp lock. "Not serious." He grinned. "The worst part is behind us. Now all we need to do is find a way up and out." They stood with their heads thrown back, gazing up at a patch of the most beautiful blue sky.

"It's like we're inside a chimney."

"Much like a chimney," Broken Trail agreed. "A long time ago, I helped a friend escape through a chimney in the middle of the night. His name was Red Sun Rising—he was a Cherokee. If he hadn't escaped, a mob would have hanged him in the morning."

"How did you and your friend escape?"

"We climbed."

"I can stand on your shoulders, then pull myself out."

He shook his head. "That hole is six feet above my head. You might be able to touch the edge with your fingertips, but to pull yourself out you'd have to get your elbows over the top. It's too high."

"No, it's not. Lift me up. I can stand with my feet on your shoulders. Then I'll jump." She stepped in front of him and faced the rock wall.

"Well, we can try." He grasped her around the waist. When he lifted her, he was amazed at how light she was. Just arms and legs.

"Higher! Keep lifting!"

He shifted his grip to her hips and raised her higher. He heard the scratch of her fingernails on the rock.

"Higher!"

Then he was gripping her about the thighs, and then about her knees, all the time pushing her up. He felt her bare feet on his shoulders and wrapped a hand around each ankle to steady her.

"Let go!" she said. "I'm going to jump."

As soon as he took his hands away, he felt the force of her feet push against his shoulders as she sprang up. Suddenly, her weight was gone. He looked up and there she was, the top part of her body out of the hole and her skinny brown legs dangling. Then her legs, too, disappeared.

For several moments, Broken Trail was staring up at a patch of empty sky. Then Rosa's head and shoulders appeared. "Where are we?" he asked.

"Above the falls."

"Are we between the river and the road?"

"No, we're on the other side of the road, away from the river. There are trees and bushes all around the hole where I climbed out, and there's a big old cedar tree right at the edge, with roots growing into the cracks in the rock."

"Do you see any people?"

"Do you mean on the road?"

"On the road or anywhere."

"I'll go look."

Broken Trail sat down to wait. He studied the rock walls, hoping to see handholds and footholds that he might use to climb up to the hole. There were very few, not nearly enough. Sitting at the bottom of the pit, he felt happy for Rosa, up there in the bright sunshine where there were trees and singing birds. Then he felt a stab of fear. What if the guards saw her? He pictured her tall, thin shape outlined against the sky. He imagined the men chasing her. Why was she taking so long?

Suddenly, the light above grew dim. He looked up, half blinded by the glaring sun behind her silhouette.

"Are you there?" she asked.

He laughed with relief. "Where else would I be?"

"There was a wagon going along the road," said Rosa. "It's gone now. The entrance to the cave is below us, but closer to the river. There are three men guarding it. I spied on them."

"What're they doing?"

"They're eating. One man is cutting slices from a whole ham. Thick slices." Broken Trail heard the hunger in her voice.

"Listen," he called. "I'm sending you to fetch a rope twenty-five feet long. When you've got it, tie knots in the rope about one foot apart. Then you'll tie one end of the rope to that cedar tree and toss the free end down into the hole. While you do that, I'll head back toward the cave and make the tunnel wider and higher wherever it's needed. I'll bring everybody here through the tunnel. We'll climb the knotted rope to escape."

"Uh-huh. So where am I supposed to get a twenty-five-foot rope?"

"From my sister. Her name is Hope. She lives partway

between Newark and Queenston, about seven miles from here. That's not too far for you to walk?"

"Of course I can walk that far. But maybe she doesn't have a rope."

"Then she can buy one at the general store in Newark. That's not a problem. Hope has enough money to buy a rope and she'll want to help."

"Are you sure of that?"

"When you meet her, you'll see for yourself." He remembered Hope's painting of the fleeing man, her readiness to hide fugitive slaves and her eagerness to share with him the money their father had hidden under the cabin floor. "Go now! You can reach Hope's cabin before dark. Spend the night there. In the morning, she'll either give you a rope or go to Newark to buy one. By sundown tomorrow, you can be back here with it. I'll have everybody from the cave gathered here, ready to escape. Then up the rope we go!"

"But I don't know exactly where your sister lives or what her home looks like."

"It's four miles beyond Queenston. She lives in a one-room log cabin. At the start of her lane, you'll see a sign nailed to a tree. 'H. Cobman,' it says."

"I can't read letters. Nobody ever taught me."

Broken Trail groaned. If Rosa were at the bottom of the pit where he was, he could show her what the letters looked like. "That doesn't matter. Just look for a cabin that has a chicken house at the back."

"Her cabin might not be the only one with a chicken house at the back."

"When a black-and-white dog with yellow eyes charges out at you, you'll know you've found the right cabin."

"You mean, I'll know it when he tears me to pieces."

"Yell at him, 'Captain, lie down!' He likely won't obey, but Hope will hear the ruckus and come to the rescue."

"I hope so! What's your sister look like?"

"Brown hair. Pink cheeks. She's fourteen, but not as tall as you or as—" He was about to say 'skinny,' but thought better of it.

"Are you telling me she's just fourteen and she lives alone, with just a dog for company? So, she doesn't take orders from anybody?"

"That's right." He smiled, aware that his voice revealed his pride in his sister.

"I want to meet her," declared Rosa. "See you tomorrow."

The shadow at the mouth of the pit vanished, leaving Broken Trail blinking at the sun in his eyes.

# CHAPTER 20

# Under Rock and River, Alone

Now he was alone. Broken Trail stared into the dark passage, which he must now re-enter. It had been midday when he and Rosa started out from the cave behind the falls—now it was midday again. If Joseph was right, Skinner's men would take the captives from the cave in two days. One of those days had already gone by.

With Hope's help, Rosa would carry out her part of the plan. By tomorrow at sundown, the knotted rope would be in place. It was up to him to carry out his part—he must have the captives here, ready to climb the rope to freedom.

It would not be easy. First, he had to make his way back to

the cave, clearing more rock along the way to make the tunnel wide enough and high enough for a tall, heavy-bodied man like Joseph to pass through. His next challenge would be to persuade the captives to follow him. Finally, he must lead them here. He must do all this by sundown tomorrow.

Broken Trail took one last look at the patch of blue above the pit. Then he raised his arms to the sky and prayed. "Invisible Spirits, guide me! Help me to bring those suffering people safely to freedom at their journey's end!"

As his prayer ended, he pressed his hand against his chest and felt the shape of the amulet he wore under his deerskin poncho. Then he dropped to his knees and entered the dark hole. At once his body blocked the light coming from behind.

The knees of his buckskin leggings had finally worn through. He felt the hardness of the tunnel's rock floor. Sharp fragments of stone cut into his skin. Rosa, he reminded himself, had crawled the whole way on bare knees, not once mentioning the harshness of the rocks. He missed Rosa: the sound of her breathing and the calmness of her voice. She was a plucky girl. When she had asked to come with him, he'd thought she would be a hindrance. How wrong he had been!

He had already raised the ceiling of this part of the tunnel. It was high enough so far. He moved carefully. A rock to the head would be a clear signal that he had work to do, but a gentle bump would do as well as a violent collision.

As he progressed, he tried to estimate how far he must go

to reach the cave. From Rosa's description of the location of the hole at the top of the pit, he figured the total distance was about one hundred yards. One hundred yards as the crow flies, that is. But they had not been flying like crows. He and Rosa may have been under the river and the rock for half again that distance. It had taken them from midday to midday. Now, making his way back to the cave, he must cover that distance in half the time.

Broken Trail crawled steadily forward. His progress was good. So far, he had already raised the tunnel roof as much as needed. Sooner than he expected, he reached the place where he and Rosa had stopped to eat their apples. This would be a good spot to rest for a few minutes. He sat down, easing his back against the tunnel wall and stretching out his legs. He wished that he had another apple and wondered where Rosa was. She may have reached Hope's cabin by now. She might, at this moment, be telling his sister about the plan.

After a short rest, Broken Trail stood up. Here, the tunnel's roof was high enough to let him walk, as long as he stooped. But soon the roof lowered, and he was again creeping forward on hands and knees. Then he felt the first drops of water fall upon his head and neck. He was back under the river.

He pulled out his tomahawk. This was the stretch of tunnel where he and Rosa had been forced to wriggle on their bellies. He set to work, thrusting the pick end of the tomahawk's head into cracks in the limestone. Every time he pulled down a chunk of rock, he imagined hundreds of tons of water breaking through. Rock fragments fell all around him. He groped for cracks into which he could shove debris out of the way.

The thunder of the falls filled his head. It was as sultry as a sweat lodge inside the tunnel. Even the water trickling through the stone was warm. Was it day or night? He had lost all sense of time. How long had it been since he last slept? He needed rest. Maybe, for just a few minutes, he should lie down on the tunnel floor. But if he did that, would he ever rise again? He struggled on, refusing to stop. Finally, his arms and legs collapsed under him.

As he lay with his cheek resting on the hard stone, a dizzy sensation came over him, and he seemed to rise out of his body so that he was in some other place. There were maple trees and birches all around. Golden sunshine dappled the ground. Then he smelled a pungent musk, heavy and familiar. From between the trees emerged a wolverine that was the size of a wolf. It approached him, its jaws open to show its yellow teeth.

"*Oki!*" he whispered.

The wolverine spoke to him in thoughts, not words, so that he heard its message not with his ears but with his mind. *Broken Trail, rise up! It is time for you to become the leader that your dream long ago foretold.*

Broken Trail breathed deeply. As he pulled the musk-scented air into his lungs, he felt his strength return. His bones, sinews and muscles were infused with power. Then the vision disappeared. The trees, the sunshine and the wolverine were gone.

He sat up and shook his head. Years had passed since the last time he saw his *oki* in its visible form. At the age of thirteen winters, he had been granted a vision that revealed the pathway of his life. In that vision, his *oki* foretold that he would be a great leader.

He took another deep breath. No smell of wolverine. He was not in a forest. He was in a tunnel under the Niagara River. Surely, there could not be much further to go. He found his tomahawk, which had fallen from his hand, rose to his hands and knees and went on.

· · ·

Broken Trail reached the cave at nightfall. It was dark, but not pitch black. The wall of water was suffused with a faint light. He could just discern the shapes of sleepers sprawled on the cave floor as he emerged from the crevice. He looked for Joseph. When he found him, he knelt to tap him on the shoulder.

"I'm back. I've found a way out."

Joseph sat up and looked about. "Where's Rosa?"

"She's gone for a rope."

Joseph had many questions, which Broken Trail did his best to answer. But sleep overcame him. He did not so much lie down as topple over while in the middle of explaining what needed to be done.

CHAPTER 21

# Who Will Follow Me?

Morning had come. Broken Trail had slept and eaten. Now he stood with his back to the wall of plunging water, shouting his message to the fourteen men, women and children who sat facing him on the cave floor. All had their eyes on Broken Trail as they strained to catch his words over the noise of wind and water.

"It's going to be dark in the tunnel. You'll bruise your knees crawling over rough rocks. You must be careful not to bump your head. At the end of the tunnel, you'll have to climb a rope. There'll be knots in the rope to help you climb. Then you'll board a boat to cross the river from Queenston to the other side." He paused, wondering whether he should try to explain the rest of the plan. Or had he said enough? From their blank expressions, he decided that he *had* said enough. More at this point would cause confusion.

When he looked into their faces, few met his eye. Some shrugged. Some looked anxious. No one looked eager. Something was wrong. When he first arrived at the cave, Joseph had welcomed him as a second Moses and used words like "wilderness" and "deliverance." But had the captives ever accepted him as a leader? His skin was pale and his eyes were blue. Despite his scalp lock, he feared they saw a white man when they looked at him.

This would not be the first time Broken Trail had faced rejection. There had been some people in his Oneida village who at first had refused to accept him. Over and over he had needed to show his courage and skill before finally winning acceptance as a warrior. So he was not surprised to find rejection here.

Today, though, he had no time to prove himself. The captives must come with him now, or not at all. He'd found them a way out. They had to take it. They had to trust him. Or would they rather remain slaves for the rest of their lives?

"Who will follow me?" he shouted. For a time, it appeared that Joseph was the only one who would. Then the eldest of the three children stood up and stepped forward. This was the boy who had been sitting apart from the crowd when Broken Trail first stumbled into the cave. He had pointed out Broken Trail's presence to the others. Now he stood alone.

He had bold eyes and the calm look of a leader, even though he was no more than eleven years old.

Seeing the boy step forward, others exchanged ashamed glances. Then two men stood up, hovering nervously behind the boy. One by one, others rose.

"What's your name?" Broken Trail asked the bold-eyed boy.

"Cato."

Broken Trail held out his hand. Cato took it firmly. The formality of a handshake felt odd, but somehow right.

"Let's go!" Broken Trail shouted. After that, a sharp look, a nod or a pointing finger was all the communication needed as the others formed a line.

"I'll go last!" Joseph's voice boomed in Broken Trail's ear. "I'm the largest person here. If I stick in a tight spot, everybody behind me is stuck. But if I'm at the end of the line, I'm the only one who doesn't go free."

They started off. Broken Trail led, followed by Cato and then the others. As they progressed through the tunnel, Broken Trail did not consider the possibility of failure or doubt for a moment that the knotted rope would be there, tied securely to the trunk of the cedar tree. In his mind's eye he saw Rosa waiting in the bushes at the top of the pit, her dark eyes shining as she peeped between the leaves.

His thoughts moved on to the next stages of his plan. He must steal Skinner's satchel and hire a boat large enough to carry fifteen persons—no, sixteen, because he would be with them. He had money to do this. Thayendanegea provided him with enough coins to meet expenses when he was on the great chief's business. But freeing slaves was not part of Thayendanegea's business. Broken Trail felt uneasy about this. Of course, he would repay the money. But the problem was not money. The problem was himself, because he knew that slavery was evil and yet he worked for a slave owner. Someday soon, he would need to deal with that.

The sudden collision of Broken Trail's head with a rock returned him to the immediate challenge of guiding four-teen human beings through a dark tunnel. He should be paying attention to the task at hand. Within a few minutes, however, he was thinking again, this time about Skinner's satchel. He must have it. How was he to get it? Thanks to Peter Shaw, he knew several things about Jonas Skinner. He knew that Skinner was a scrawny little weasel of a man. He also knew that on Skinner's visits to Queenston he stayed at a disreputable inn called Berry's Tavern, owned by a man notorious for dealing in every sort of evil that money could buy.

Broken Trail's best chance of getting his hands on Skin-ner's satchel was to rent a room at Berry's Tavern. To carry out his plan, he would pretend to be as bad as any villain who chose that nest of evil for his lodging. Although nothing in his training as a warrior had prepared him for this challenge, his skills in diplomacy would be useful. As for his appear-ance, his scalp lock and his Oneida clothes could help to create the right image. Some white men who lived among the Native people—*coureurs de bois*, traders and adventurers of various kinds—were far from saints. Many were downright scoundrels. So scoundrel was the role he would play. He'd been a student. He'd been a warrior. He was about to add actor to the list.

A cry from behind him interrupted his thoughts.

"Stop!" someone shouted. "There's a problem!"

Broken Trail halted. "What is it?"

There was a babble of voices distinct from the rumble of water over their heads.

"A woman collapsed."

"Who?"

"Dolly, the little girl's mama."

"Is she dead?"

To Broken Trail, it sounded all too possible that someone had died from the heat in the tunnel. But the woman had merely fainted. After a few minutes she regained consciousness and was revived with an apple. The line moved on.

Now Broken Trail came to the low and narrow passage where it was necessary to crawl. Dragging his rifle and his carrying basket took all his attention until at last he reached the open space where he could look up to see daylight and, hanging from above, a knotted rope.

# CHAPTER 22

# Escape

As soon as Broken Trail was up the rope and out of the pit, he saw Rosa waving to him from the bushes. He waved back. Then he gave Cato a hand and stayed at the top of the pit to help others climb out.

"Be very quiet!" he warned as they emerged. "We're near the road. If travellers are going by, they must not hear us."

The last person to climb from the pit was Joseph. The journey through the tunnel had splotched his red velvet livery with grey rock dust. Although there were several rips in the cloth and one shoulder was half torn off, he looked victorious. Joseph and Broken Trail shook hands, grinning triumphantly. Then Joseph looked away, his eyes searching the bushes and trees. When he caught sight of Rosa, he ran to her with open arms.

Broken Trail hauled up the knotted rope, untied it from the trunk of the cedar tree, coiled it and laid it on the ground.

"Listen!" He spoke in a voice just loud enough for all to hear over the noise of the falls. "We're at the top of the escarpment. The entrance to the cave is at the bottom. I'm going to see if the guards are there and what they're doing."

Between the top of the pit and the edge of the gorge was the Niagara Portage Road. Before crossing it, Broken Trail looked both ways. The road was empty. When he reached the edge of the gorge, he crouched low so that his shape would not stand out in silhouette against the sky. From this vantage point he could see right to the bottom.

The three guards were in clear view, lounging comfortably as they smoked their pipes. Two were leaning against the limestone slab. The tall, shambling man, the one who had been asleep, was sitting on a rock with his long legs stretched out ahead of him. Broken Trail smiled. What a surprise that lay in store for those men when they discovered that the captives had disappeared from the cave!

He hurried back to the captives. "Do you remember a great stone slab standing in front of the entrance to the cave?"

A few nodded, but the rest shook their heads. Broken Trail figured that they'd had other things on their minds while being dragged past the slab and through the fissure in the rock that gave entry to the cave.

"Before long, Skinner's men will go into the cave to bring you out and ship you across the river to sell at a slave market. If they don't do it today, they'll do it tomorrow. Here's my plan. We have eight strong men who can topple that slab so that it will block the entrance. You men will stay here. Keep a close watch on the guards. As soon as they go into the cave, you must rush down there as fast as you can to knock over the slab. If it doesn't completely block the entrance, there are plenty of loose rocks you can use to plug any gaps."

"Ah!" A sigh of appreciation rose from all sides as people caught his meaning.

After a pause, Broken Trail continued. "As soon as Skinner's men discover that their captives aren't in the cave, they'll rush back to the entrance. They won't be able to get out that way, because you'll have it blocked. Of course, they'll soon realize there must be another way out. To find it will take some time. They'll come to a few dead ends, but sooner or later they'll discover the tunnel we used."

Everyone nodded. There were excited whispers.

"They'll follow the tunnel to the end, but the knotted rope won't be there." He pointed to it lying coiled on the ground.

Laughter bubbled from the crowd. "It will serve them right if they never get out."

"Yes! Serve them right! Let them starve down there."

"It would serve them right," Broken Trail agreed. "But sooner or later, they'll manage to escape. If one of them stands on the shoulders of that very tall fellow, he can lift himself through the hole. He'll go for a rope, just as Rosa did, so they can all climb out. Then they'll have to report to Skinner to tell him what happened. By the time they've done that, we'll be across the river in New York State. So here's what you men have to do as soon as you have the cave entrance blocked. You must scatter into the woods and make your way to Queenston. Bring the rope with you. Don't go into the town. Hide in the forest. Watch the landing place. That's where you'll board the boat to cross the river. The women and children will join you later, when I have everything arranged."

Dolly, the woman who had fainted in the tunnel, objected. "Skinner will send slave catchers to round us up. It won't matter which side of the river we're on. Even if the catchers don't get us, there'll be plenty of white folks happy to turn us in for the reward."

Apart from the rumble of the falls, there was silence while Broken Trail told them about Mr. Skinner's satchel and the bills of sale. He explained the loophole in the new law, which made it necessary for them to leave the province of Upper Canada in order to come back as free people. It was complicated, and it didn't make sense to them. He explained the loophole a second time. It still didn't make much sense, but finally he convinced them that it would work.

"What will the rest of us do while the men wait to knock over the big slab and you go off to steal Mr. Skinner's satchel and hire a boat?" the fair-skinned woman asked.

"You'll go with Rosa to my sister Hope's cabin. She'll hide

you. Her cabin is partway between Queenston and Newark. You can stay there until I have a boat hired."

Rosa nodded. "Hope will feed us. She keeps chickens. There'll be fresh eggs and delicious chicken soup. The night I stayed with Hope, she had a big pot simmering over the fire."

At the mention of food, the children's eyes grew round as saucers. The women smiled.

"Keep inside the cover of the trees along the road," Broken Trail warned. "Don't let anyone see you." He watched the women and children vanish into the shelter of the bushes.

Broken Trail shouldered his rifle. "You all know what you have to do. I'm going now to get Skinner's satchel and rent a boat."

# CHAPTER 23

# Berry's Tavern

~

Berry's Tavern was a two-storey building with a roofed porch across the front. The clapboards had once been white, but most of the paint had worn off. From the edge of the roof hung a wooden sign on which an emblem of three strawberries and a single leaf was crudely painted.

Broken Trail approached the door and pressed the latch. A jangle of bells startled him as he opened the door. Stepping inside, he realized that Berry's Tavern had once been a trading post, for it had the kind of wide counter where Native hunters stacked the bundles of pelts that they brought to trade. There was no trace of furs or trade goods now. On the counter, a brandy cask, a rum keg and a big beer barrel rested on cradles.

Six small tables with chairs filled the room. Behind the counter were two doors, one open and one closed. From the room with the open door came the clatter of pots and pans and the smell of roasting meat. A man wearing a checkered shirt came through the doorway. He was thin and white-faced, with sparse hair and cold eyes. He looked at Broken Trail the way everybody did, taking in the scalp lock and the deerskin clothes.

"What can I do for you?" the man asked.

"I'm looking for a place to stay. I've been told that Berry's Tavern will suit me well."

"You've been told, eh? Who did the telling?"

An alarm bell rang in Broken Trail's head, reminding him of one of the first lessons of diplomacy: never reveal anything unless it gives you an advantage. "A friend."

"Fair enough. Here's our rates. Shared bed in the common bedroom, one penny. Private bed, two pennies."

"What about a private room?"

The man raised his eyebrows. "Six pence a night."

Expensive! But he needed privacy in order to carry on his investigation. "I'll take the private room."

"Show me your money."

Broken Trail pulled a small purse from his pouch. He took from it a sixpence, which he set spinning on the table nearest to him. The man deftly picked up the coin, still spinning, from the table.

"That's for one night." Broken Trail looked the man straight in the eye. "I may be here for more. I'll pay each night separately, in advance. Keep my account for food and drink to pay at the end."

"I'm Frank Berry." He gave Broken Trail a thin-lipped smile that did nothing to alter the coldness of his eyes. "I'll show you your room."

Broken Trail followed Berry to a narrow staircase. On the way, he noticed blotchy, discoloured patches on the tavern's grimy floor. Old bloodstains. His fingers tightened on the handle of the knife he wore in his belt.

At the top of the staircase, Broken Trail peered through an open doorway at eight cots, each with a grey blanket folded at its foot. The common room. He followed Berry along a hall, passing five closed doors. At the sixth, they stopped. Berry flung open the door. "This one's yours." His manner seemed to say, *Take it or leave it.*

"It will do." The room had a bed with dusty curtains and a dirty coverlet. Awfully unkempt for sixpence, but it would have to suffice for Broken Trail's purposes.

Berry nodded. "Leave it the way you found it." He left him to explore his room.

Behind a privacy screen, a chamber pot with a cracked lid rested on the floor. There was one chair, which was missing a spindle from its back. The room had a wooden wardrobe with a door that sagged on its hinges, a washstand with a pitcher and a chipped bowl and, above the washstand, a mirror that had lost much of the silvering on its back. Everything in the room was worn, bent, stained or slightly broken.

Broken Trail opened the dirty casement window and looked out. His room was at the front, overlooking the porch. *It will do*, he said again, this time to himself. If necessary, he could make a quick exit out the window and over the porch roof. The roof had a downward slope from which he could leap easily to the ground.

Turning from the window, he set his rifle against the wall and shrugged his carrying basket off his back. In it were his best deerskin clothes with bright beadwork and long fringes. He had brought these garments with him from Brant's Ford in case Lieutenant-Governor Simcoe should invite him to attend a formal occasion where it would be important to look like a young chief. An impressive appearance might not be important at a place like Berry's Tavern, but the very squalor of the room made him want to clean himself up. The clothes he was wearing were just as grimy as his present surroundings, and his leather leggings were completely out at the knees. He checked the pitcher on the washstand. It was full of water. He could wash himself and trim his scalp lock before changing into his good clothes. Broken Trail set to work. As he was dressing, he heard the bell at the door downstairs jangle several times. From below he heard male voices and the occasional shout.

When he was satisfied with his appearance, he left the room, taking neither his rifle nor his carrying basket with him. As he passed the common bedroom, he noticed that one of the beds now had an occupant, a man who lay stretched out in ragged clothes, sound asleep. Broken Trail started down the staircase and then stopped halfway to survey the scene, hoping to see a man with a brown leather satchel held by a strap over his shoulder. He was not there.

The room was half full. At the table closest to the staircase, four men were playing cards. There was money and a jug of rum on the table. The players were hard-looking men. They looked up at Broken Trail with unwelcoming curiosity and then returned to their game.

At the table closest to the kitchen, two men were eating. One was sawing at a slice of well-done roast. On the other's plate was a slab of something grey and unidentifiable. Both plates held boiled potatoes and cabbage. They were eating industriously, pausing only to drink from the tankards at their places.

Three men sat at the table closest to the front door. Two of them were quarrelling. They both looked like ordinary working men, wearing homespun shirts and short jackets. One spoke in a low growl, the other responding in shrill, protesting outbursts. The growler seemed to be goading the other. The subject of their dispute was not clear. The only words Broken Trail heard clearly were "...lazy as the rest of her tribe."

The third man was older than the others, and differently dressed. His clothes, when new, had been expensive. Their shabbiness showed that they had seen better days, for the velvet of his russet frock coat was worn down smooth to the underlying cloth and his white cravat was limp and creased. He looked disgusted with his quarrelling companions.

Broken Trail sat down at an unoccupied table. After a short time, a sturdy woman wearing a stained apron came from the kitchen to take his order. The meat choices were roast of ox and boiled salt pork. Broken Trail asked for the roast of ox. When it came, he wished that he had not. To have flesh so tough and stringy, the ox must have toiled for many years pulling wagons on the Niagara Portage. Hunger kept Broken Trail chewing until his jaw ached. He had given up and set down his knife when the bell over the door jangled.

The man who entered was small in stature, with narrow shoulders. He wore a short coat and breeches. He paused just inside the door and looked around. His eyes were like the eyes of a cat: luminous, opaque and watchful. Over his shoulder was slung a brown leather satchel.

# CHAPTER 24

# Skinner's Leather Satchel

Broken Trail picked up his knife and returned to his abandoned dinner, pretending to give the leathery meat his full attention while directing sidelong glances toward Skinner. Skinner sat down at an empty table beside the quarrelling men. Broken Trail noticed Skinner's satchel disappear under the table, while the strap remained in the crook of his elbow. He must be holding the satchel on his lap.

Berry came from the kitchen with a glass of brandy on a tray and set it in front of Skinner, who nodded his acceptance. When Berry returned to the kitchen, the woman who had waited on Broken Trail came out. Maybe she was offering

Skinner the choice of roast ox or boiled salt pork. Whatever it was, he shook his head and then spoke briefly to her. She returned to the kitchen. Skinner sipped his brandy, glancing occasionally at the two men quarrelling at the table next to his. The woman came back with a plate of bread and cheese, which she set at Skinner's place.

The disturbance continued. Broken Trail was still pretending to work on his slice of roast ox when the man sitting with the quarrelsome pair abruptly left their table and came over to join him. He sat down, leaned back in his chair and gave Broken Trail the kind of smile that could quickly turn into a snarl.

"I've seen you before. You work for Joseph Brant."

Broken Trail put down his knife. "I might."

"Brant's a deep one. I hear he's been making himself a fortune selling off parcels of land that the British government gave to the Six Nations. From all appearances, he pays you pretty well for a messenger boy."

This was more than Broken Trail's pride could take. "I'm his deputy, not his messenger boy. I represent Captain Brant at conferences. I help negotiate treaties."

"I see." The man looked amused. "So if the old chief stays at an inn, you stay at an inn. Those are pretty fine clothes you're wearing—those fringes and beads. You're all dressed up like a warrior."

Broken Trail made no response. He was thinking he might try a couple more chews of the roast ox when suddenly the man's hand shot up and Broken Trail saw the shiny point of a knife blade nearly touching his eye. He stared at the man and made no move. Slowly, the man drew his knife back.

"Ha-ha! I just wanted to see what kind of warrior you are." He looked disappointed that Broken Trail had not flinched.

"Now you know."

The room was hushed. Broken Trail felt all eyes upon him as he rose from his chair, leaving the man with the knife sitting alone. One of the players at the card table said, "Bold fellow!" in an approving way. Slowly and deliberately, Broken Trail sat down at Skinner's table. Skinner greeted him with a slight nod.

The quarrelling pair resumed their dispute. Broken Trail, now closer to them, could not avoid overhearing some of their words. The deep-voiced man was enjoying himself, giving sly grins as he uttered words like "savage," "squaw" and "dirty." The victim of his abuse looked at him with a hatred he made no attempt to hide.

Skinner cast a contemptuous glance in their direction. "Those two are headed for trouble. Fred married an Indian. I don't know why he had to do that, but the rest of us leave it alone. Bill loves to goad Fred until he loses self-control." He watched thoughtfully. "It could lead to bloodshed. I hope not. This is a good place to do business. A man getting killed in a brawl makes it bad for everybody."

Berry came from the kitchen carrying a tray loaded with drinks. He frowned as he watched Bill and Fred. Then he looked at the old bloodstains on the floor.

The growling man, Bill, said something that sounded like

"maggoty meat." Whatever it was, it tipped Fred over the edge. He leapt to his feet and drew his knife.

"Drop the knife!" Berry shouted. He set down his tray on the counter.

Skinner watched without expression, like someone more accustomed to observation than action.

"Drop the knife!" Berry shouted again. It was too late. Fred lunged. Men from every table clambered to their feet, chairs overturned.

"The fools!" Skinner muttered. He sprang to his feet and jerked his satchel from under the table. The satchel was swinging from his arm when he grabbed Fred's shoulder.

*Not wise*, Broken Trail thought. *That's not how you stop a man with a knife.*

Fred whirled about, his blade flashing. Turning too quickly, he lost his balance. As he stumbled, his knife descended and the blade entered the flesh of Skinner's upper arm, narrowly missing the satchel strap.

Fred pulled his knife from Skinner's arm. Blood spurted. Broken Trail jumped up, grabbed Skinner and helped him to a seat. With his knife, he cut the sleeve of Skinner's shirt. He gripped Skinner's arm and pressed both thumbs just above the wound. Blood covered Broken Trail's hands. The satchel, splattered with blood, was right under his nose.

People were all around him, crowding close. "Go for a surgeon!" Berry shouted.

Broken Trail heard the server complain that the murder of a customer was bad for business, especially the murder of a regular customer. "Wife, he's not dead yet," Berry snapped.

Broken Trail's thumbs stayed pressed against the artery. All the while, his eyes were on the blood-covered satchel. Skinner's left hand, white-knuckled, clutched the strap as if his life depended on it.

Broken Trail felt the onlookers' eyes upon him. He overheard their comments but did not look up. "That Indian knows what's he's doing," one man remarked. "Skinner's better off with him than with Old Cut Bones dressing the wound."

"I don't think he's an Indian," said another.

"Where do you think he comes from?" asked someone else.

"He's from Six Nations land on the Grand River." Broken Trail recognized the voice of the man in the shabby frock coat. "He works for Joseph Brant. They're in some crooked business together."

Broken Trail pretended not to hear this. Such a story suited his purposes. He was seen as a scoundrel in the company of scoundrels, just as he had planned.

By the time the surgeon arrived, Broken Trail had stopped the bleeding. The crowd made way as he entered the inn and approached the scene.

"Step aside, young man," the surgeon ordered. Willing enough to leave Skinner in the surgeon's hands, Broken Trail obeyed. He saw that Skinner's grip on the satchel's strap was as strong as ever. The surgeon examined the wound.

"How is he?" Berry asked.

"Grave. Very grave. The quantity of sanguinary discharge may in itself prove fatal. Nonetheless, I fear lest coagulation lead to febrile exuberance of the pulse, to prevent which I shall open an orifice in the left arm in order to withdraw some twenty ounces of blood. Unless this is done, mortification may set in."

Broken Trail, not understanding a word, marvelled that the surgeon could make so much of a simple stab wound. The woman scurried into the kitchen to fetch a bowl. Although Broken Trail knew that Skinner had already lost more blood than was good for him, he made no comment. Let white man's medicine do its best! The satchel had his full attention now.

"Remove the patient's shirt," the surgeon ordered.

"No! No!" Skinner pleaded. Despite his protests, the shirt was torn from his back and the satchel from his hand. By the time the surgeon's thin blade descended to pierce Skinner's vein, the satchel was lying on the floor, kicked under the table.

"My satchel! My satchel!" Skinner moaned as he lost consciousness. He sounded as though he were calling to a loved one far away.

How was Broken Trail to get that satchel now? It lay undefended under a table, but there were a dozen people in the room.

The surgeon had not yet finished. While the woman carried away the bowl of blood, he bandaged Skinner's arm. "I shall return tomorrow to dress the wound and, if necessary, apply a fomentation to the affected part. For now, the patient must be put to bed. When he is strong enough, feed him thin gruel if he desires to eat."

After a stretcher had been improvised from two poles and a blanket, Skinner was laid upon it. Two men wrestled it up the narrow staircase, followed by the crowd. Broken Trail noticed that the crowd no longer included Fred and Bill, both having quietly left the tavern by this time. Only Broken Trail, the surgeon and the woman were still downstairs. The surgeon and the woman were earnestly discussing other foods that Skinner might safely eat. The satchel was still lying under the table.

"Look!" Broken Trail pointed at the satchel. "There's that satchel he cares so much about. I should take it up to him."

"Yes, do!" The woman smiled. "That would be so kind!"

Broken Trail retrieved the satchel and bounded up the stairs. He walked straight by the open door where the crowd had gathered around Skinner, who now lay on his bed. Entering his own room, Broken Trail picked up his carrying basket and his rifle. He lowered these carefully out the window onto the porch roof. As he climbed out, he heard a weak voice coming from the open window of Skinner's room.

"My satchel! My satchel!"

Broken Trail felt like laughing. Under his breath, he murmured, *I've got it right here.*

# CHAPTER 25

# Ten Bills of Sale

∽

Alone on the road, Broken Trail gave a whoop and did a little war dance—just a few steps, lifting his knees and stamping his feet—until he laughed at himself for the silliness of it and sensible thoughts took over.

Although the waning moon was only a sliver, he could see the road well enough. He was tempted to open the satchel, just to make sure of its contents. But it would be smarter to wait until he reached Hope's cabin. The women and children hiding there would be overjoyed to see him.

Or would they be? It was the middle of the night. Everyone would be asleep. Hope's wolf-dog would be sitting on the front step, keeping watch. Broken Trail pictured a mass of shaggy hair and sharp teeth hurling itself at him with frenzied barking. No. This was not a good idea. He'd better find a quiet place to curl up with the satchel and wait until dawn.

On reaching the H. Cobman sign, he took a few steps up the lane. Still outside a dog's hearing range, he crawled under the low branches of a spruce tree and lay down on the carpet of fallen needles. The roof of branches angled above him. Accustomed to snatching sleep where he could, he dozed off with his rifle and carrying basket beside him and the satchel cradled in his arms.

• • •

A blue jay's shriek roused him at first light. He crawled from under the spruce branches, stretched and headed up the lane, with the satchel's strap over his shoulder. When he neared the cabin, Captain announced his arrival with a flurry of barks and growls that brought Hope to the door.

"Quiet!" she commanded.

The dog obeyed. Through the open door, Broken Trail saw the faces of her guests hovering anxiously behind her. When they recognized him, their worried looks turned to smiles.

"I knew it must be you." Hope grinned. "Rosa has explained the plan. Did you get the satchel?"

"Here it is." As he stepped inside, he unslung it from his shoulder and held it out to her. She touched the leather and pulled her hand back.

"There's blood on it."

"Skinner's blood."

"Did you ...?"

"No. I didn't harm him. There was a ruckus at the tavern. He was hurt."

"Have you looked inside?"

"Not yet."

He laid the satchel on the table. Everyone crowded around, jostling to get a good view. The rising sun, shining through the little panes of glass in Hope's window, cast a shaft of light directly on the satchel.

Two buckles and a brass lock latched it shut. Broken Trail undid the buckles and used his tomahawk to wrench open the lock. Inside the satchel were two fat envelopes and a small leather-bound writing case. On one of the envelopes was written "Bills of Sale," and on the other, "Boat."

"Everybody, please sit down." Broken Trail pulled out the "Bills of Sale" envelope.

When all were seated, two on Hope's rickety chairs and the others on the floor, he opened the envelope and pulled out a sheaf of papers. He counted them. There were ten papers, all bills of sale. Quickly, he flipped through them to check the dates. Every sale had taken place after July 9, 1793.

"These are exactly what we need. This is the evidence that is going to prove you're free. I'll call out the names on these papers, even the men's names, just to be sure there's a full list. Tell me if I call your name."

"Louis." No answer. He picked up the next paper. "Henry." No answer. He picked up the next. "Mandy." He stopped. This was the first name he recognized, and Mandy was dead. After a moment of silence, he set that paper aside and continued. "There are two names on this next one, Mary and Tobias."

"That's us." The speaker was the fair-skinned woman. She was sitting on one of the chairs with her little boy on her lap. "Please read me what it says."

Broken Trail read aloud. "Received from Jonas Skinner. One hundred and fifty dollars, New York money. Of which one hundred dollars represents the purchase price of the mulatto woman Mary, and fifty dollars the purchase price of her son Tobias, a quadroon five years of age. Signed, Robert Benson. Dated July 12, 1793."

"Thank you." The woman looked to the floor. "I am Mr. Benson's daughter and Tobias is his grandson. I thought we'd be worth more than that."

Everyone stared at Mary and Tobias. Hope clapped her hand to her mouth. Her expression showed the same horror that Broken Trail felt. How could a man sell his own daughter and grandchild as if they were property? But they *were* his property. It was heartless. Unnatural. Like slavery itself.

Broken Trail cleared his throat and turned to the next bill of sale.

"Cato."

The bold-eyed boy who had stepped forward first to enter

the tunnel raised his hand. "That's me, and I want to read it myself!"

Surprised voices erupted. "Can you read?"

"Who taught you to read?"

"Smart boy!"

He started at the top and read clearly and confidently straight through to the end. He was Cato, eleven years old, sold to Jonas Skinner by Thomas Bradley for ten pounds, Montreal money. Signed at Newark, Upper Canada, July 11, 1793.

Cato finished reading. "This is the first thing I've ever read out loud."

Broken Trail did not hide his curiosity. "How did you learn to read?"

"I taught myself. A wealthy family bought me when I was two years old to be raised as a personal slave for a boy my own age, Master William. This was in Charleston. It was against the law to teach a slave to read and write. But nobody cared if I looked at Master William's picture book. One page had a picture of a cow, and the word 'cow.' That's how I began. When Master William started school, I'd wait till he was playing with his white friends or riding his pony. Then, when my chores were done, I would read his books and look over the lessons lying on his desk. I learned just about everything he learned at school. This lasted for three years. Then Master William was killed. When he grew too big for the pony, his parents bought him a horse. He was teaching his horse to jump over fences when he fell off and broke his neck. After he died, there was no place for me in that household. The family sold me. The people who bought me were Loyalists, so they had to leave South Carolina. I had a couple of other owners after that. The last one was Mr. Bradley. He brought me from Halifax to Newark. None of my owners ever knew that I could read."

"Can you write as well?" asked Broken Trail.

"I think I can. Many times I held a pen in my hand and wrote in the air. I never dared to make a mark on paper. If somebody saw it, then my secret would be known." He turned to Broken Trail with a look of friendly cunning. "That doesn't matter any longer, does it?"

"You don't need to hide it any longer, but it does make a big difference, because as soon as you are free, you can—"

The sentence remained incomplete, for at that moment there was a knock at the door. Everybody looked about nervously. Hope opened the door. In walked one of the men who had remained behind to topple the limestone slab. He was a short, stocky man with skin as dark as ebony. He was wearing ragged breeches and a torn shirt.

"Louis!" a woman called out, looking pleased to see him there.

All eyes turned toward him. "Hello, Louis!"

"We did it." He leaned against a wall, slightly out of breath. "The guards are in the cave and the entrance is blocked. We pushed over the slab. It left a small gap on one side, but we filled it with big rocks. It would take days for three men to clear them out of the way. My fellows have gone to Queenston to hide in the woods. I'm on my way to join them."

Broken Trail took back the bill of sale that Cato had read. "We'll finish looking at these later. I need to see what's in the envelope marked 'Boat.' I must know what it says, because I have to go to Queenston to make arrangements for a boat." He turned to Louis. "Stay for a moment. Before you leave, you'd better hear what's in the envelope, so you can tell the other men."

CHAPTER 26

# Human Cargo

∽

The envelope marked "Boat" contained one sheet of paper and a bundle of banknotes. Broken Trail looked first at the paper. He read silently. When he had finished, he read aloud.

"This paper is a contract between Jonas Skinner and William Ulmer. Ulmer will provide a bateau and crew to ferry sixteen Negroes and three guards across the Niagara River from the landing at Queenston to the landing on the New York side. Total cost: ten dollars. Deposit paid: one dollar. Balance due upon sailing: nine dollars. The contract says that the bateau will be at Queenston Landing, ready to load, at 11:00 p.m. on July 22." He looked up. "Hope, what's the date today?"

"July 22."

"Are you sure?"

"Of course. I have a schedule for delivering fresh eggs to the Officers' Mess at Navy Hall. I need to keep track of dates."

So this was the very day! But he shouldn't be surprised. Two days ago, there had been enough food in the barrels in the cave to last about two days. So it made sense that the bateau would leave tonight. Broken Trail looked again at the contract, mumbling audibly. "Total cost: ten dollars. Deposit paid: one dollar. Balance due: nine dollars." He flipped through the banknotes. "Nine dollars. It's all here."

Everyone stared at him, and he read in their eyes the question he was asking himself: *What are we going to do?* In a flash, he knew the answer.

"The boat is already arranged. Skinner expected to have a cargo of sixteen slaves to ferry over the river. That included Mandy, so now it's fifteen. The contract says: three guards. Well, those guards won't be there. Even after they find their way out of the tunnel, they still have to report to Mr. Skinner to tell him that his cargo has disappeared. So what do we do at eleven o'clock tonight?"

"We take the boat!" Cato shouted.

Broken Trail nodded. "We have the nine dollars right here to pay the owner."

One of the women had doubts. "What if Skinner shows up?"

"He won't. First, because he just handles the money and leaves the rough work to his men. Second, even if he wanted to, he won't be strong enough to leave his bed. He lost a lot of blood."

Louis spoke next. "Look! The contract says three guards. If we show up at the landing without any guards, the boat owner will think we're a bunch of runaways. If we offer him the money, he'll think we stole it. Instead of taking us across the river, he'll call the constable to lock us up."

"You're right. We need three guards. I can be one. There are two men in Queenston I can ask to help us. Two plus me equals three."

"You!" Some laughed, others shook their heads.

Rosa summed up what everyone appeared to be thinking. "Moses, in your Indian clothes, with all those beads and fringes, you just don't look like a guard."

"If I borrow some ordinary clothes and a hat to cover my scalp lock, and if all three of us carry guns, then surely it would be believable."

Heads nodded. "It may work."

"It *will* work! The boat owner won't care who the three guards are. The contract just says 'three guards.'" He turned to Louis. "Here's the plan. When the bateau looks ready to load, it'll be eleven o'clock. Stay in hiding until I arrive with the other two men. When we march you onto the bateau, act as though all the miseries of the world were heaped upon you. If we seem to treat you badly, remember it's just pretending." He paused. "Do you have the knotted rope?"

"Yes. We brought it with us."

"While you wait in the woods, untie the knots and cut the

rope into lengths long enough to bind a man's wrists. It will look more convincing if we herd you onto the bateau with your hands tied behind your backs."

When Louis had left the cabin, Broken Trail handed the bills of sale to his sister.

"Hope, will you finish reading these to the others? I must go to Queenston right now to talk to the two men I told you about. They both hate slavery. They'll help us. Can you find your way to Queenston Landing tonight? Do you know where that is?"

Rosa stood up. "I do. Don't worry. I can get us there on time."

"You brought everyone safely here, so I'm sure you can."

Now Broken Trail picked up the small writing case, the third thing that had been in the satchel. It was about ten inches long, five inches wide and two inches thick. The binding was smooth leather.

"Cato, look at this!"

Broken Trail opened the case. The interior was lined with red velvet. Fitted into precisely formed spaces were two well-trimmed quills, a small pen knife and a tiny, sealed jar of ink. "Do you want to try writing something?" he asked Cato. "I'm sure my sister can find a piece of paper for you to use." Cato stared at the writing case, his eyes round. Broken Trail closed it and held it out to him.

"This is yours."

The boy's mouth twisted and tears rolled down his cheeks as he took the writing case from Broken Trail's hands.

# CHAPTER 27

# Plans and Preparations

❦

Hope flipped through the papers in the envelope. "They need a safe way to carry their bills of sale."

"Why not pockets?" Dolly suggested. "I'm a seamstress. I can sew a pocket in a trice. A pocket attached to a waistband can be hidden under your clothes."

"I have cloth, thread and needles," said Hope. "Who else knows how to sew?" Other women put up their hands. Hope pulled a wicker box from under her bed. "There's work for all of us, because we need one pocket for each bill of sale. Let's have a pocketing bee, like a quilting bee, while we wait for my brother to arrange the boat."

Broken Trail nodded. "Perfect! If anybody's challenged to

prove he isn't a slave, he can just pull the bill of sale from his pocket. If he's arrested, he can show the magistrate the date on the bill of sale. It will prove that the loophole in the new law has made him free."

He turned to Cato, who was inspecting his new writing case on the floor. "Cato, here's a task for you. Teach everybody to recognize the letters that make up their name so they can point to it on their bill of sale. When you've done that, make sure that each bill of sale goes to the right person." Cato, holding fast to his writing case, beamed with pleasure and pride.

Broken Trail turned to his sister. "Cato can bring the men's pockets to the landing." He picked up his carrying basket. "Hope, I have my old deerskin clothes in this basket. I'll change into them and pack in the basket these fine clothes I'm wearing right now. I'll leave the basket in your care till I return."

He undid the leather ties that bound each legging to his belt and slipped his poncho over his head. In a very short time, he was ready to leave. Hope followed him to the door, where they stood facing each other.

"You and I found each other at just the right time," she said.

"Yes. The very day the new law was passed. Now we'll work together to free people left in slavery."

"Fate meant us to be allies. Brother and sister. Cut from the same cloth."

"So we are," he agreed. "As soon as this part of the battle is won, I'll be back to tell you about our victory. And we'll have other stories to share."

"You can tell me what it was like to live with the Oneidas."

"You can tell me about growing up in the barracks on Carleton Island."

"But first, we have work to do. Before you leave, I have something to give you." She reached into a slit in the side of her gown, where she wore her own pocket, and pulled out a handful of coins. "Here's some of the money Pa hid under the floorboards. You refused it before. Now you must take it. You're bound to have expenses before these folks are free."

He did not refuse. "Thank you." He put the coins into his pouch. He gave her a hug—the first hug he had given his sister since she was a tiny baby, when Ma had let him hold her.

He left her to hand out cloth, needles and thread for the pocketing bee.

• • •

Peter Shaw was weeding the vegetable patch in front of his cabin when Broken Trail approached. From inside the cabin came the clackety-clack of a spinning wheel.

"Hello!" Broken Trail greeted him.

Shaw raised his head, straightened his back and rested the head of his hoe on the ground.

"Well, look who's here!" He and Broken Trail shook hands. "Have you found the folks you were looking for? The man and the girl?"

"I found them and thirteen more slaves that Jonas Skinner plans to ship across the river tonight. I helped all of them escape. Now, with some help from you, there's a way they can become completely free under the new law."

"Let's go indoors while you tell me about it."

When they went inside, Mrs. Shaw stopped her spinning and rose from her stool. "Welcome back! I'll make us some tea."

"Thank you, Mrs. Shaw, but I'm sorry, there's no time for that. Jonas Skinner has a boat hired for tonight to take slaves across the river to sell in the United States. I need your husband's help to use that boat as part of a plan to free them."

"Whoa! Start at the beginning." Shaw took a seat and gestured for Broken Trail to join him. "First, please, where did you find the man and his daughter and all those other people? Where was Skinner hiding the slaves he bought up?"

Broken Trail sat beside him. "In a cave behind the falls."

"What!"

"Yes. A big cave. I found the trail leading to the entrance, and then I found another way out—"

"I've heard stories about a cave. You mean to say they're true?"

"There certainly is a cave. It's like a dungeon with three walls of rock and one of water. If any of the captives look too weak or sick to fetch a good price at the slave auction, Skinner's men throw them out of the cave to die on the rocks under the falls."

Shaw nodded. "So that's how those bodies got into the river. We pulled out another one yesterday. A woman. The river had pulled all the clothes off her body, except for a bandage on one leg."

"Her name was Mandy. I put that bandage on her leg. She was a prisoner in the cave. Skinner's men threw her out because of her bad leg."

"Those people are even more evil than I imagined. They must be stopped."

"You can help. And so can your friend who owns the shed."

"His name is Roger Counter. Before we go to ask his help, you'd better tell me the rest."

"As I said, I found another way out of the cave. All the captives escaped through it. We trapped their guards in the cave. Tonight, we're going to use the boat that Skinner hired. This is where you can help. I have with me the contract for the boat rental. It says there will be three guards. So you and I and Roger Counter will pretend to be guards."

"Just a minute! You have the contract? How did you get your hands on that?"

"I stole Skinner's satchel." Broken Trail took from his pouch the envelope labelled "Boat" and pulled out its contents. "Here's the contract and here's the money. The only other thing I need is a disguise."

"I'll lend you some of my clothes. You can wear my hat to hide your scalp lock."

"How can I help?" asked Mrs. Shaw.

"While we're gone, my dear, please bring out some of my clothes for Broken Trail to wear." Shaw rose from his chair. "Let's go talk to Roger. You can explain the rest to both of us together. Night will soon be here."

# CHAPTER 28

# Light in Darkness

∾

They found Roger Counter in his cornfield, checking the silk tassels of the ripening corn. He was the gruff-voiced man who had provided his shed as a resting place for the bodies pulled from the river. Counter listened, cursing under his breath while Broken Trail explained how the slaves had been thrown from the cave.

"We buried another one yesterday." Counter clenched his fists.

"I know. Peter told me. He's sure you'll want to help. It will take only two hours of your time to give fifteen enslaved people freedom for the rest of their lives."

"What do we need to do?" asked Counter.

Broken Trail explained the plan as the sun set over the cornfield. When he had finished, Counter said, "I understand. Peter, you and I will pretend to be guarding a shipment of slaves because the contract for the boat rental says there'll be three guards."

"That's right. As soon as we disembark on the American side, you and Peter can go back to Queenston any way you like. I'll guide the captives through the bush to Fort Niagara, and in the morning, I'll hire boats to take them back across the river. As soon as they set foot in Upper Canada, they'll be free."

"Sounds fine. I'll do it."

"It's nearly dark," said Shaw. "My wife likely has those clothes ready for Broken Trail to put on."

"There won't be a moon tonight." Counter glanced skyward as they left, walking between the tall rows of corn. "I'll meet you at the landing when the first stars appear."

"Bring your rifle," said Broken Trail.

. . .

Back in Peter Shaw's cabin, Broken Trail studied his reflection in the looking glass that hung on the wall. What a transformation! The young man wearing Shaw's black, broad-brimmed hat was a different person from the Oneida warrior with his scalp lock and shaved pate.

"I'd hardly know you!" Mrs. Shaw nodded approvingly.

Shaw picked up Broken Trail's ordinary clothes and packed them into a rucksack. He slung his rifle over his shoulder by its strap.

As Broken Trail and Shaw walked down to the landing, lightning flashed eerily on the far shore. It was heat lightning. No thunder. It didn't feel like rain. There were no ships on the river, only a few small boats pulled up on the bank.

Soon it was completely dark. Shadows between the trees transformed into pools of darkness where anything might lurk. Every sound—night birds, mosquitoes, frogs—was distinct and sinister. The prickling at the back of Broken Trail's neck told him he was being watched. From that feeling he knew that the fugitives were already there, waiting. When, one by one, they stepped out from the darkness, their dark faces could be seen only by the shining of their eyes. He recognized Rosa by her white gown.

Cato came up to him. "Everything's ready. I've given the men their pockets with the bills of sale."

"Well done!" Broken Trail patted him on the back.

When the first stars appeared, Roger Counter joined them, carrying his rifle. Louis had begun to tie the men's wrists with the lengths of rope. "Tie them loosely," said Broken Trail, "so they can easily pull their hands free."

The splashing of oars broke through the dark night. For a moment, everyone held their breath. The bateau's hull bumped against the wharf with a soft thud. By the light of the stars, Broken Trail saw the mast with the crossbar intended for a square sail, but the mast was empty. There were six oarsmen to row the boat. The owner, William Ulmer, stood in the cargo area.

"Present your papers," he whispered, his voice hoarse. Broken Trail stepped from the wharf onto the deck of the bateau and held out the contract for Ulmer to inspect, although he suspected that the night was too dark for him to read a word of it. Ulmer's eyes went straight to the price line. "Nine dollars. Before we sail."

"No. Four now, and five when we get there." Broken Trail handed over four banknotes.

Ulmer took them. "As you wish." He looked again at Broken Trail. "Where's the giant?"

"Pardon?"

"The tall man who usually handles the money."

"There's been a change of crew."

"Is that so?" He paused, leaving a moment of silence. "Why didn't Skinner get in touch with me? He wouldn't send a different crew without letting me know."

"Skinner had an accident. He's not well."

Ulmer looked past Broken Trail at the figures standing in darkness on the landing. "I don't like the way you have those Negroes tied. Binding their wrists isn't secure enough. They should be bound hand and foot, the way Skinner always has them ready to load."

"It didn't seem necessary. Tonight there's just fifteen, not a full load. We can handle them this way."

"It's not safe." Ulmer leaned forward, peering closely at

Broken Trail. "I don't know you. I don't know what's going on. But I smell a rat. Here's your money back. I'm not taking those Negroes across the river. Now I thank you to get off my boat."

Broken Trail took one step back, swung his rifle from his shoulder and pointed it at Ulmer's chest. "We're taking over the boat."

"It's piracy. You'll hang for this!"

"Men!" Broken Trail shouted to Shaw and Counter. "Cover the rowers, and get everybody on board double-quick!"

Their hands quickly freed, the fugitives swarmed on board. Broken Trail made a quick count to be sure everyone was there.

"Cast off!" he shouted. The rowers looked bewildered, but obeyed, anxiously eyeing the rifle. Broken Trail kept it pointed at Ulmer as they pulled away. "Change course. We're going to Fort Niagara."

"You have no right!" Ulmer roared.

"This gun gives me the right," declared Broken Trail.

Shaw had his rifle pointed at the oarsmen on one side of the bateau, and Counter at the oarsmen on the other side. With a swirl of water, the bateau turned and headed north.

*Perfect!* Broken Trail smiled with satisfaction. Instead of guiding fifteen people on a seven-mile walk through the bush, he would let the bateau carry them to Fort Niagara, where they could sit on the grass below the ramparts and wait for morning.

The river's strong current left the rowers with nothing to do but dip their oars from time to time to maintain a steady course. The stars were still shining when the bateau docked at the landing below the bastions of Fort Niagara. Broken Trail shouldered his rifle and took from his pouch the five dollars still owing. He gave the banknotes to Ulmer.

Ulmer gripped the banknotes in his fist without bothering to count. "Skinner's going to hear about this," he snarled.

"I'm sure he will." Broken Trail smiled, knowing that it would be an interesting conversation.

When all passengers had left the bateau, it cast off again, this time back up the dark river toward Queenston. Now fighting against the current, the rowers leaned into the oars.

CHAPTER 29

# The Day of Jubilee

⤸

"It's a warm night, and there's no need to hide." Broken Trail stepped from the wharf. "We can rest here on the grass until morning. When the sun rises, we'll see Newark right across the river."

The air radiated with the music of a late summer night, with crickets chirping in counterpoint with a chorus of frogs. There was no moon, but the stars were bright. Rosa stared into the darkness across the river, where Mr. Steele's house stood on a bluff overlooking the river. After a long silence, she sighed. "Mama's over there. She's waiting for us."

Broken Trail smiled reassuringly. "It hasn't been long, only a fortnight since you saw her last."

Joseph's gaze was in the same direction. "No time at all. Deliverance for Rosa and me is coming sooner than I imagined possible. For Sukie, it will take much longer. But Rosa and I will be able to see her from time to time, when Mr. Steele is away at work." He paused. "I'll work hard to earn the money to buy her freedom. There are good people in Upper Canada, people who'll pay a fair wage whatever the colour of a man's skin."

"What kind of work will you seek?" Broken Trail asked.

"Work in a stable. Grooming. Training. I'm good with horses. But I'll do any honest labour that comes my way."

"Me, too," added Rosa. "Maybe I can be indentured, like your sister was. Then I'll have room and board during my indentures, and money at the end. Hope thinks that indentures are nearly as bad as slavery. But I don't think so. With indentures, you know exactly when it's going to be over."

"It will all work out. We'll never stop being a family, even when we're apart." Joseph turned to Broken Trail. "The first step is to cross the river. How are we going to do that? It's too far to swim."

"All day, people go back and forth between Newark and Fort Niagara. It's mostly by rowboat or canoe. When the fish aren't biting, a fisherman may come to the wharf to pick up a fare to earn a few pennies that way. Then there are the Mohawks who have a settlement outside Fort Niagara. If it weren't dark, you'd see their canoes pulled up on the riverbank. When George Washington sent an army to destroy all the native villages in New York Province, hundreds of people fled to Fort Niagara. That was thirteen years ago, but some Mohawks have remained. They make their living by hunting to supply the officer's mess with game and by ferrying people across the river. It's a poor life, compared with what they once had in the Mohawk Valley."

"Have you money to pay them?" Joseph asked.

"Yes. My sister gave it to me."

Rosa yawned and stretched out on the grass. All around them, others were already asleep, some adding their snores to the chirping of the crickets and the croaking of the frogs. Before long, only Broken Trail remained awake. He sat cross-legged on the dry grass, keeping watch.

• • •

At sunrise, the blast of a bugle jolted the sleepers awake. Reveille. Across the river at Navy Hall soldiers were raising the red, white and blue Union flag of Great Britain.

Joseph jumped to his feet. "Blow, bugle, blow!"

"Blow, bugle, blow!" Everyone joined in the joyous shout.

Shaw and Counter, who had been shouting with the rest of the group, approached Broken Trail.

"That surely was a change of plans last night!" Shaw yawned.

"It was a sudden idea. When I saw we'd have to take over the bateau, I thought we might as well spare ourselves the seven-mile walk through the bush to Fort Niagara."

Counter grunted. "I'm not worried about Ulmer going to the law about it, not when ninety per cent of what he does with that boat is illegal. He couldn't identify us anyway. It was too dark."

Shaw nodded. "As soon as you return the clothes I loaned you, Roger and I will head back through the bush to the landing on the New York side. Before we take the ferry to Queenston, we'll pay a visit to our abolitionist friends. We'll tell them about last night's work. They'll be encouraged by what we've done."

"With a bit of organization, abolitionists on both sides of the border can work together to help enslaved blacks escape to freedom," said Counter.

Broken Trail pulled out his deerskin clothes. "What's needed is a network of safe houses where fugitive slaves can hide."

"We'll start working on that," Shaw replied.

"So will I." Broken Trail smiled. *Hope and I will work together*, he thought.

After Shaw and Counter left, Broken Trail watched the first boat of the day approach from the Upper Canada side of the river. It was a rowboat coming from Navy Hall. Its passengers were two soldiers, their red coats bright spots of colour in the morning mist. The rowboat docked at the wharf. When the soldiers had disembarked, the rower shipped his oars and sat waiting, his boat bobbing gently.

Broken Trail hurried down to the wharf to negotiate with him. For one penny, the man would carry two adults and one child. Before long, another rowboat from Navy Hall reached the landing. When the passengers had disembarked, Broken Trail made a similar arrangement with the boatman.

When Broken Trail finished talking with the second boatman, he saw a group of warriors carrying paddles over their shoulders on their way to the river, where overturned canoes lay on the bank. The warriors' clothing was part leather and part cloth, and all of it shabby. Their rags made him glad that his leather leggings were only worn out at the knees. He raised his arm in greeting, and they answered his salute.

One warrior stepped forward. "You are dressed like a Six Nations warrior, but your eyes are blue and your skin is pale."

"I am a warrior of the Oneida Nation, although I was white by birth."

"Who are these black people with you?"

"They are slaves who escaped from their owner. In Upper Canada, there's a new law that will make them free as soon as they have crossed the river. I see that you have good canoes. I can pay one penny for each ordinary canoe to carry two people and three pennies for a freight canoe large enough for six passengers."

The warriors spoke briefly among themselves. Then the warrior who had been their spokesman answered for them all. "The money is good. We are glad to earn it in this way, for it is right for warriors of the Six Nations, who have lost so much of their land and power, to lend a hand to people who have lost everything."

.  .  .

The dew on the grass was barely dry when they all set off.
Broken Trail was the last to embark. In the little flotilla were
Mohawk warriors paddling canoes, white settlers rowing
rowboats, and fifteen black men, women and children on
their way to freedom.

The distance across the Niagara River was no further than
a cannon ball could fly. Yet it meant the difference between
slavery and freedom—and these were worlds apart. As the
flotilla neared the Upper Canada shore, Joseph, somehow el-
egant in the remains of his red velvet livery, led the singing,
in which everyone joined:

> *Blow ye the trumpet, Blow*
> *The gladly solemn sound.*
> *Let all the nations know*
> *To earth's remotest bound,*
> *The Year of Jubilee is come.*

CHAPTER 30

# The Trail Goes On

Later that morning, Broken Trail found Lieutenant-Governor Simcoe in his headquarters at Navy Hall. He was sorting papers into piles. On the floor were stacks of maps, books and documents, which a young ensign was carefully putting into packing boxes.

Simcoe raised his head when a sentry ushered Broken Trail into the room. "Welcome back! You see me in the midst of packing to leave Newark. I have determined that this town is too close to the United States border to serve as the capital of Upper Canada.

"Where will the capital be?" asked Broken Trail.

"Toronto."

"Toronto! There's nothing at Toronto but a fort, a few huts and mud."

"That will change, and so will its name. The capital of Upper Canada will be called York." He paused. "But you and I have other business to talk about." Simcoe dismissed the ensign, telling him to take twenty minutes for a cup of tea.

As soon as Simcoe and Broken Trail were alone, Simcoe's face turned serious. "Did you find those two slaves, Joseph and his daughter, that you were looking for?"

"I did. And I made use of the loophole that you told me about. This morning I brought back as free men and women not only Joseph and Rosa but thirteen others that a jobber had hidden with them."

Then he told Simcoe about the cave behind the falls and how he had led the slaves through the tunnel. He shared almost the entire story, but thought it wise not to mention to the King's representative that he had seized by armed force the bateau that the jobber had hired. This might be seen as an act of piracy. The King, as Broken Trail remembered, was not above the law.

"Those fifteen people were fortunate. Such a happy outcome is bound to be rare. Because of the difficulty, few will find freedom in that way." Simcoe shrugged his shoulders. "Partial success is better than none. I wish I had succeeded in abolishing slavery completely in this province. In time, it will happen, not only in Upper Canada but throughout the

British Empire. Right now, abolitionists in Britain and the United States are working to end the Atlantic slave trade. They're pressing England's Parliament and the United States Congress to pass laws to stop the transportation of Africans captured for sale into slavery. The work of abolitionists will end the slave trade within the next ten years. But it will still leave thousands of people enslaved on this side of the Atlantic."

"To free those people will be my work." Broken Trail sat up straight. "It will start right now. I'm on my way to Brant's Ford to tell Captain Brant that I still share his dream of uniting the Native people in one federation, but I can no longer work with him unless he frees his slaves."

"Oh!" Simcoe gasped. "You know what that means."

"It means that I'll no longer be his deputy."

"You'll be on your own."

"No. I know others who'll work with me. Two men who live in Queenston. My sister."

As Broken Trail was speaking, the ensign returned. He saluted and stood at attention. "Shall I pack another box, Lieutenant-Governor?"

"Ah, yes. Be especially careful with the maps."

"I see that you're very busy," said Broken Trail. "I shall take my leave."

They shook hands. Broken Trail promised to visit the Lieutenant-Governor in York if his travels should take him there.

. . .

Broken Trail reached Hope's cabin that afternoon. His plan was to stay just one night while on his way to Brant's Ford. As it turned out, he was still there two days later, for he and his sister had fourteen years of catching up to do.

She told him about her childhood in the Fort Haldimand barracks on Carleton Island, and about her year in the orphan asylum after their mother's death, and about the four months she spent as an indentured servant. She described the journey she made after her indentures were cancelled, in search of her family, and how their father, at his death, had left her his cabin and the land that had been granted to him as a Loyalist.

Broken Trail told her how Oneida hunters had found him, a nine-year-old runaway sleeping in a pile of leaves in the forest, and taken him to their village. She listened, fascinated, to his account of life in the longhouse and his struggle to become a warrior accepted by all. He told Hope about his *oki* and about his mystic dream and the prophecy that when he died, all nations would mourn.

"For a long time, I thought this meant the white nations and the nations of the people who adopted me." He looked up at Hope's painting, hanging on the wall, of the black man running on a moonlit road. "But now I see that my vision meant more than that. All my life I'll continue to seek justice for the people who first lived on this land, but I'll not rest until there's justice for black people, too."

"We can work together to free slaves. We'll start now. You must find others willing to hide runaways. You and I can build a network of safe houses, like stagecoach stops on the way to freedom."

"Hope, we've already started. We began when you took in the fugitives that Rosa brought to you."

"Thank you for sending them here."

"I'll send you more. Be ready."

## ABOUT THE AUTHOR

Jean Rae Baxter is the descendant of settlers who arrived in New France in the 17th century, Loyalists who came here in the 1780s, and immigrants from Germany in the 19th century. There were many family stories to awaken her interest in writing about Canada's history.

Jean Rae Baxter's previous novels have been Canadian Book Centre "Best Books for Kids and Teens." She received the Hamilton Arts Council Award for Young Adult Literature and the City of Hamilton Heritage Award. Her books have been shortlisted for the Ontario Library Association's Red Maple Award and British Columbia's Stellar Award. In the U.S., she won both the Gold and Bronze Moonbeam Awards, and received an Honourable Mention at Boston's New England Book Festival.

In preparation for writing, she likes to travel to the places where her novels are set. For *The Knotted Rope*, she visited the Cave of the Winds behind Niagara Falls several times, and experienced the wall of falling water, the wind and the thunderous noise. She visits many schools and libraries to talk about Canadian history and conduct creative writing and family history writing workshops.

If you would like to contact her, her email address is jeanraebaxter@cogeco.ca. You may reach her on Facebook at www.facebook.com/JeanRaeBaxterBooks.